东方智慧丛书

The Wisdom of the East Series

The Wisdom of the East Series

东方智慧丛书

Editors-in-Chief: Tang Wenhui　Liu Zhiqiang

主编：汤文辉　刘志强

Academic Adviser: Zhang Baoquan

学术顾问：张葆全

Chinese-English

汉 英 对 照

Selections from the Classic of Poetry

诗经选译

Compiled and Commented by Chen Piwu

选释：陈丕武

Proofread by Zhang Baoquan

中文审读：张葆全

Translated by Shen Fei

翻译：沈菲

Illustrated by Yin Hong　Guan Ruilin　Liu Rong

绘图：尹红　关瑞琳　刘荣

· 桂林 Guilin ·

GUANGXI NORMAL UNIVERSITY PRESS

广西师范大学出版社

图书在版编目（CIP）数据

诗经选译：汉英对照 / 陈丕武选释；沈菲译；关瑞琳，尹红，刘荣绘．—桂林：广西师范大学出版社，2018. 9
（东方智慧丛书 / 汤文辉等主编）
ISBN 978-7-5598-0714-4

Ⅰ．①诗… Ⅱ．①陈… ②沈… ③关… ④尹… ⑤刘… Ⅲ．①古体诗－中国－春秋时代②《诗经》－译文－汉、英 Ⅳ．①I222.2

中国版本图书馆 CIP 数据核字（2018）第 045145 号

广西师范大学出版社出版发行
（广西桂林市五里店路 9 号　邮政编码：541004
网址：http://www.bbtpress.com）
出版人：张艺兵
全国新华书店经销
广西广大印务有限责任公司印刷
（桂林市临桂区秧塘工业园西城大道北侧广西师范大学出版社集团有限公司创意产业园内　邮政编码：541100）
开本：880 mm × 1 240 mm　1/32
印张：10.5　　字数：190 千字　　图：50 幅
2018 年 9 月第 1 版　　2018 年 9 月第 1 次印刷
定价：78.00 元

总　序

文化交流对人类社会的存在与发展至关重要。季羡林先生曾指出，文化交流是推动人类社会前进的主要动力之一，文化一旦产生，就必然交流，这种交流是任何力量也阻挡不住的。由于文化交流，世界各民族的文化才能互相补充，共同发展，才能形成今天世界上万紫千红的文化繁荣现象。[1]

中国与东盟国家的文化交流亦然，并且具有得天独厚的优势。首先，中国与东盟许多国家地理相接，山水相连，不少民族之间普遍存在着跨居、通婚现象，这为文化交流奠定了良好的地理与人文基础。其次，古代中国与世界其他国家建立起的“海上丝绸之路”为中国与东盟国家的经济、文化交流创造了有利的交通条件。

中国与东盟诸多使用不同语言文字的民族进行思想与文化对话，

[1]季羡林：《文化的冲突与融合·序》，载张岱年、汤一介等《文化的冲突与融合》，北京大学出版社，1997年，第2页。

自然离不开翻译。翻译活动一般又分为口译和笔译两类。有史记载的中国与东盟之间的口译活动可以追溯至西周时期，但笔译活动则出现在明代，至今已逾五百年的历史。

在过去五百年的历史长河中，东盟国家大量地译介了中国的文化作品，其中不少已经融入到本国的文化中去。中国译介东盟国家的作品也不在少数。以文字为载体的相互译介活动，更利于文化的传承与发展，把中国与东盟国家的文化交流推上了更高的层次。

2013 年 9 月，国务院总理李克强在广西南宁举行的第十届中国—东盟博览会开幕式上发表主旨演讲时指出，中国与东盟携手开创了合作的“黄金十年”。他呼吁中国与东盟百尺竿头更进一步，创造新的“钻石十年”。2013 年 10 月，习近平总书记在周边外交工作座谈会上强调要对外介绍好我国的内外方针政策，讲好中国故事，传播好中国声音，把中国梦同周边各国人民过上美好生活的愿望、同地区发展前景对接起来，让命运共同体意识在周边国家落地生根。于是，把中华文化的经典译介至东盟国家，不仅具有重要的历史意义，同时还蕴含着浓厚的时代气息。

所谓交流，自然包括“迎来送往”，《礼记》有言：“往而不来，非礼也；来而不往，亦非礼也。”中国与东盟国家一样，既翻译和引进外国的优秀文化，同时也把本国文化的精髓部分推介出去。作为中国最具人文思想的出版社之一——广西师范大学出版社构想了《东方智慧丛书》，并付诸实践，不仅是中国翻译学界、人文学界的大事，更是中国与东盟进行良好沟通、增进相互了解的必然选择。广东外语外贸大学和广西民族大学作为翻译工作的主要承担方，都是国家外语非通用语种本科人才培养基地，拥有东盟语言文字的翻译优势。三个单位的合作将能够擦出更多的火花，向东盟国家更好地传播中华文化。

联合国教科文组织的官员认为，“文化交流是新的全球化现象”。[1]我们希望顺应这一历史潮流与时代趋势，做一点力所能及的事。

是为序。

刘志强

2015 年 1 月 25 日

[1]《联合国教科文组织文化政策与跨文化对话司司长卡特瑞娜·斯泰诺的致辞》，载《世界文化的东亚视角》，北京大学出版社，2004年，第3页。

Preface to The Wisdom of the East Series

Cultural exchanges are of significant importance to the existence and development of human society. Mr. Ji Xianlin once pointed out that cultural exchange was one of the major driving forces for the progress of human society. It is inevitable that communications and exchanges will occur among different cultures. As a result, the interaction and mutual enrichment of cultures contribute to the formation of a diversified world featured by cultural prosperity.[1]

The cultural exchange between China and ASEAN countries, in the trend of mutual communication and interaction, also boasts of its own unique strengths. First of all, China borders many ASEAN countries both by land and by sea, and intermarriage and transnational settlement are common, all of which lay a solid foundation for cultural exchanges. In addition, the "Maritime Silk

[1] Ji Xianlin, "Preface to Cultural Conflicts and Integration", in *Cultural Conflicts and Integration*, edited by Zhang Dainian, Tang Yijie, et al. Beijing: Beijing University Press, 1997, p.2.

Road" developed by ancient China and other countries has helped pave the way to a smooth economic and cultural exchange between China and ASEAN countries.

People from China and ASEAN countries use different languages. Thus, to conduct a successful dialogue in the cultural field requires the involvement of translation and oral interpretation. Historical records show that the oral interpretation among people of China and ASEAN can be dated back to the Western Zhou Dynasty (1122-771 B.C.). It is also known that translation started to boom in the Ming Dynasty, which was five hundred years ago.

In the past five hundred years, a large number of Chinese cultural works were translated into many languages of ASEAN countries and many of them have been integrated into their local cultures. China has also translated a lot of works of ASEAN countries. Translation is beneficial to inheritance and development of culture and upgrades the cultural exchanges between China and ASEAN to a higher level.

As Mr. Li Keqiang, Premier of the State Council of the People's Republic of China, pointed out in his speech at the opening ceremony of the 10th China-ASEAN Expo held in Nanning in September, 2013, China and ASEAN jointly created "10 golden years" of cooperation. And he called on both sides to upgrade their cooperation to a new level by creating "10 diamond years". In October, 2013, General Secretary Xi Jinping emphasized, in a meeting with Chinese diplomats, the importance of introducing China's domestic and foreign policies to other countries and regions, and making Chinese voice heard in the world. Xi also pointed out that "Chinese Dream" should be connected with her neighboring countries' dream of a better life and with the development prospect of those countries so as to build up a community of shared destiny. Against such a backdrop, it's of both historical and current significance to translate Chinese classics and introduce them to ASEAN countries.

Exchanges are reciprocal. According to *The Book of Rites*, behaviors that do not reciprocate are not consistent with rites. Like ASEAN countries, China has had excellent foreign cultural works translated and introduced domestically, and also translate and introduce to the outside world the essence of local culture and thoughts. Guangxi Normal University Press, one of the top presses in China that focus on enhancing the influence of the humanities, made the decision to publish *The Wisdom of the East Series*. It is not only a big event in Chinese academia, but also a necessary choice for China and ASEAN to communicate with each other and enhance mutual understanding. Guangdong University of Foreign Studies, and Guangxi University for Nationalities, the main undertakers of the translation project, are both national non-universal languages training bases for undergraduates and boast strengths of ASEAN languages. Cooperation between the two universities and the press will surely facilitate dissemination of traditional Chinese culture to ASEAN countries.

UNESCO officials hold the belief that cultural exchange is a new phenomenon of globalization.[1] We hope that our efforts could breathe the spirit of this historical momentum and help ASEAN countries understand Chinese culture better.

Liu Zhiqiang

January 25, 2015

[1] "Speech of Katerina stenou, Director of Division of Cultural Policies and Intercultural Dialogue", from *East Asia's View on World Culture*. Beijing: Beijing University Press, 2004, p.3.

诗经选译

Selections from the Classic of Poetry

前　言

《诗经》是中国最早的一部诗歌总集。它产生的年代，大约上起西周初年（公元前 1046 年），下至春秋中叶（约公元前 500 年），历时五百多年。它产生的地域主要在黄河流域，但远及江汉流域。

《诗经》的编撰结集，有采诗、献诗、删诗三种说法。周代设有采诗的专官到民间采诗，目的是通过这些诗了解施政的得失和各地的风俗；当时大量的民歌和贵族的诗篇，就是依靠采诗献诗制度得以保存下来的；周代有乐官，这些乐官不但保管诗，且负担教授诗、乐的任务，诗都有乐调，诗乐不分，这些加工编辑工作，可能就是由乐官太师完成的。

《诗经》收录的诗歌分为风、雅、颂三大类。关于它的分类标准，后世学者有不同的看法，其中比较普遍的看法是按音乐分类。古人所谓“风”，即指声调而言，有十五国风，就是十五个不同地方的乐调。有大雅、小雅。雅是秦地的乐调，周秦同地，这地方的乐调，被称为中原正音。有商颂、周颂、鲁颂。颂即古代的“容”字，就是表演的意思。颂不但配合乐器，用朝廷声调歌唱，而且是兼有扮演、舞蹈的艺术。古人将风、雅、颂和《诗经》赋、比、兴的表现手法并称为“诗之六义”。

《诗经》思想内容涉及社会生活的方方面面。国风诗，多为抒写人们恋爱、婚姻、家庭生活，也有的反映人民劳动生产，还有部分诗作表现反对剥削压迫、揭露讽刺统治者丑行以及战争；雅诗中还有叙述周人开国的诗篇，被后人称为“史诗”；颂诗都是歌功颂德的作品，它和雅诗中歌颂统治阶级和祭神祭祖的诗一样歌颂祖先、神明。

《诗经》作为一部乐歌总集，在中国文学史上占有极其重要的地位，在艺术上也取得巨大的成就。首先是它的现实主义精神，从各个方面描写了我国两周数百年的社会现实生活。其次是赋、比、兴的艺术表现手法。所谓“赋”，指的是一种铺陈直叙的表现方法。所谓“比”，即是比喻或比拟，用形象的事物打比方，使被比喻的事物生动形象，真实感人。所谓“兴”，就是托物起兴，先用他物起头，然后借以联想，引出诗人所要表达的思想感情。再次是重章叠句和以四言为主的句式。重章叠句，即各章词句基本相同，只是更换中间的几个字，反复吟唱。《诗经》中的诗句，基本上是四言句式，少量诗句能突破此定格，在整齐中显现参差错落之美。最后是丰富生动、简练形象的语言。大量使用双声字、叠韵字、重叠字，丰富多彩、生动准确地表现了各种事物及其变化特征，也使诗歌富于形象美和音韵美，增强了诗歌语言的艺术魅力。

《诗经》在中国思想文化史上也具有重要的意义。大致表现在四个方面，即尊先祖、隆礼乐、崇道德、尚中和。中国文化是伴随着农耕经济的长期延续而形成的，农业文明重视经验，易于形成恒久的观念，培养起祖先崇拜的情怀。他们认为死去的祖先的灵魂仍然存在，并且对子孙后代的生存状态有影响。因此有祭祀祖先以祈求福报、叙述先民艰辛以表彰功业的传统。《周颂》是周人祭祀、赞美祖先的诗歌，《商颂》是祭祀商朝祖先的诗作。这些崇拜祖宗和祭祀先祖的传统绵延至今。

礼乐的起源，与人类文明的演进是同步的。中国的文化，非常重视礼乐。礼就是指各种礼节规范，乐则包括音乐和舞蹈。隆礼是期待尊卑长幼有序，隆乐是希望人们关系和谐。《诗经》对礼乐的宣扬，有反映恋爱、婚姻的轻松乐曲，也有反映统治者违背礼乐的歌乐，但最显著的是事神、祭祖的典仪，这些赞颂祖先和神明的乐歌大多庄重肃穆。

殷人尊天事鬼，周人代殷后，强调以德配天，以德服众，追求君子人格。《诗经》中有大量篇幅称赞周人的德行，其中最有代表性的人物就是周文王。他修明德行、施行仁政、亲睦诸侯，为西周大业的形成奠定了基础。

中国人认为人类社会和自然界所组成的宇宙，是一个生生不已、有机联系的和谐生命统一体，事物内部贯通、和合、平衡才能发展，视“和”为宇宙的本然和内在精神。这种思想形成了中国人重视整体、讲求调和、崇尚中庸的思维方式。《诗经》尚中和思想较多表现为情感表达的“温柔敦厚”，有部分诗歌在情感表达上大胆直露、忿激怨怼，但许多诗作表达情感均能恰如其分、淳正平和，即使怨愤之情，也多用理性来化解，达到和谐淳美之境。

本书选录《诗经》有代表性的诗100句（章），原文以《毛诗正义》为据，进行释析、翻译，以期能反映这部经典的风貌。

Preface

The *Classic of Poetry* is the oldest existing collection of Chinese poetry dating from the early years of the Western Zhou period (1046 B.C.) to the middle of the Spring and Autumn period (500 B.C.). Spanning over 500 years, most of the poems were produced at the Yellow River Plain and some of them were from as far as the Yangtze River valley and Han River region.

The compilation of the *Classic of Poetry* was made through collecting poems, offering them to the court and deleting improper ones. Officers were dispatched by the Zhou Dynasty court to collect poems local to the territorial states of Zhou, which the sovereign believed could help him to understand the successes and failures of his administration and local customs. A large quantity of folk songs and poems written by the aristocracy were kept in this way. As music officials of the Zhou Dynasty were in charge of keeping poems and teaching both poems and music and as poems were accompanied with music, it's possible that the compilation of poems was made by them.

Poems in the *Classic of Poetry* are classified into Airs, Hymns and Eulogies. Scholars of the later generations have different opinions on its classification standard, but the general idea is to classify it according to its music. According to the ancients, Airs referred to tones. Fifteen Airs were tones of 15 different areas. Hymns included Lesser Court Hymns and Major Court Hymns. Hymns were the tone of Qin and as Zhou and Qin were in the same place, the tone of the place was the standard tone of the Central Plains. Eulogies included Eulogies of Zhou, of Lu and of Shang. Eulogies referred to performances, so they were not only accompanied with music and sung with the court tones, but also integrated acting and dancing. The ancients grouped Airs, Hymns and Eulogies as well as expression techniques of exposition, comparison and affective images in the *Classic of Poetry* as six principles of the classic.

The *Classic of Poetry* covers all aspects of social life. The Airs speak of love and courtship, marriage and family life, farming and housework, and political satire and protest and soldiers on campaign. Poems praising the founders of the Zhou Dynasty in the Hymns are called epic poems by the later generations. Poems in the Eulogies extol merits and virtues. Like the poems in the Hymns eulogizing the ruling class and used in sacrificial rites, they praise ancestors and divinities.

As the collection of poetry, the *Classic of Poetry* occupies an extremely important position in China's history of literature, and has great artistic achievements. Its importance is first reflected in its realistic character. It describes the various aspects of social life of the Zhou Dynasty.

Second, its importance is reflected in the artistic expression techniques of Fu, Bi and Xing. Fu refers to exposition, which is straight narration or description; Bi refers to comparison, including simile and metaphor. By making a comparison, vividness is highlighted. Xing refers to affective images. By mentioning other objects in the beginning, the poet expressed his real feelings through associative links. Third, its importance is reflected in repetition and its four-line stanzas. By repetition, lines of each stanza are almost the same except for few changes of the middle characters. Most of the stanzas in the classic are four lines. Variations are shown in similarities. Last, its importance is reflected in its vivid and concise language. The vast use of alliteration, assonance and reduplication vividly depicts different objects and their change and adds artistic charm to the poetry language.

The *Classic of Poetry* also occupies a vital position in China's history of thought and culture. Its importance is reflected mainly in the following aspects: showing respect for ancestors, giving prominence to rites and music, attaching great importance to morality and advocating harmony and the doctrine of the mean. Chinese culture is formed with the development of the agrarian economy. Experience is important in the agrarian economy, so it's apt to generate the idea of respecting ancestors. People living in the agrarian economy believed that the souls of the deceased would stay with their descendants and exert influence on them. Therefore, they had the tradition of holding sacrificial ceremonies to glorify their ancestors' accomplishments and pray for their blessings. Poems in the Eulogies of Zhou and of Shang were used by the Zhou and Shang people to make sacrifices to and worship their ancestors. The tradition of making sacrifices to and worshiping ancestors has been maintained.

The rise of rites and music is in sync with the evolution of human civilization. Chinese culture highly values rites and music. Rites refer to proprieties, etiquette and codes of conduct while music includes music and dance. By valuing rites, the seniority rules are expected to be observed. By valuing music, harmonious interpersonal relationship is expected to be established. There're many poems reflecting the rites and music in the *Classic of Poetry*. For example, poems about love and marriage have sweet melodies. There are also poems that reveal violation of rites and music by the rulers. Most of the poems are about offering sacrifices to and worshipping divinities and ancestors and they are with solemn melodies.

People of Shang worshipped Heaven and offered sacrifices to the deceased while people of Zhou, the dynasty that followed Shang stressed morality and valued character of a noble man. A large number of poems in the *Classic of Poetry* praised the moral conduct of Zhou people, especially King Wen of Zhou who laid a foundation for thriving of the Western Zhou Dynasty by emphasizing moral conduct, exercising benevolent governance, and establishing harmonious relations with its vassal states.

Chinese hold the belief that the universe composed of both human society and the nature is a harmonious unity of life with endless vitality. Development is fostered when harmony is achieved. Harmony is the nature and essence of the universe. Based upon such ideas, Chinese people attach much importance to unity, harmony and the doctrine of the mean. Harmony and the doctrine of the mean in the *Classic of Poetry* are reflected in its modest expression of feelings. Some poets were blunt and bold in expressing their feelings and outraged in voicing their anger, but most of them were modest in expressing their feelings and treated their anger with rationality for the purpose of harmony.

The *Selections from the Classic of Poetry* has selected 100 representative poems and interpreted and translated them based upon the *Commentaries on the Mao Poetry* in the hope that the original classic can be presented to its readers.

目　录

Contents

詩經選譯

关雎

Fish Hawks

1. 关雎

【原文】

关关雎鸠，在河之洲。窈窕淑女，君子好逑。

《诗经·周南·关雎》首章

【释文】

雎鸠关关地鸣叫，双双栖息在河中的小岛上。那位纯洁漂亮的好姑娘，她是我追求的好对象。

【解析】

这是写一个青年男子对采集荇菜的女子的爱慕之情。诗共五章。这个女子温柔娴淑，令男子一见钟情。男子在追求采荇女的过程中，因为“求之不得”而睡不着觉，又设想以钟鼓、琴瑟取悦这位淑女，这反映了中国古代重视礼乐文化的传统。

1.Fish Hawks

Singing merrily, a pair of fish hawks inhabits the islet. The beautiful and kind-hearted girl, she is the one I seek.

From the 1st stanza of *Fish Hawks, Odes of Zhou, Classic of Poetry*

【Commentary】

The poem expresses the love of a young man for the girl who is picking leaves of nymphoides peltatum. The poem has five stanzas. The girl is beautiful and graceful, so the young man falls in love with her at first sight. The man suffers insomnia for failing to win the love of the girl, so he decides to please the girl with drums and ancient zithers, which reveals the tradition that the ancients highly valued rites and music.

詩經選譯

卷耳

Field Chickweed

2．卷耳

【原文】

陟彼高冈，我马玄黄。我姑酌彼兕觥，维以不永伤！

《诗经·周南·卷耳》三章

【释文】

我骑马登上高高的山冈，马儿都累得生病了。我把酒杯斟满酒，用来排解心中深沉的忧伤！

【解析】

这是一位贵族妇女思念丈夫的诗歌。诗共三章。这一章写到她因为思念而心中非常悲伤，无奈之下，骑马登高望远，希望能超越空间的束缚而看到丈夫；又喝酒来麻醉自己，以暂时忘记思念的痛苦。中国人讲究饮酒有节，目的是防止过量饮酒伤身或酒后失礼。但人们也经常以过度饮酒的方式来表达喜怒哀乐，喜乐太甚，无酒不足以抒其情；忧伤深沉，无酒不可以消其愁。

2.Field Chickweed

I ride my horse and climb to the top of the high hill. My horse is so exhausted that it becomes sick. I fill up my cup with wine and deal with my grief with it.

From the 3rd Stanza of *Field Chickweed*,

Odes of Zhou, Classic of Poetry

【Commentary】

The poem depicts the lady of a noble family who misses her husband. The poem has three stanzas. In the quoted stanza, such a story is told: distressed by missing her husband, the lady rides her horse and climbs to the top of a high hill, hoping to see her husband. As she cannot see her husband, she turns to wine, hoping to temporarily relieve her pain of missing him. Chinese are modest in drinking wine for fear that excessive drinking will harm health and lead to breach of etiquette. However, people often express their great rejoicing and deep sorrow by drinking excessively for they don't think they can feel their joy or deal with their grief without wine.

3．桃夭

【原文】

桃之夭夭，灼灼其华。之子于归，宜其室家。

《诗经·周南·桃夭》首章

【释文】

桃树生长得茂盛繁荣，枝头开着鲜艳的桃花。这个姑娘要出嫁了，希望你和顺地对待你的夫家。

【解析】

这是一首祝贺新婚的诗歌。诗共三章。诗中以灿烂红艳的桃花起兴，比喻新娘美丽健康的容貌。诗歌后两章以果实累累的桃树，比喻新娘将会为男家多生贵子，使其家庭人丁兴旺、和睦幸福。中国古人的观念是多子多福，所以，诗歌从这个角度来赞扬新娘。

3.Lovely Peach Blossoms

How lovely peach blossoms are! Peach trees are in full blossom. My girl, you are going to get married. I hope you will kindly treat your husband's family.

From the 1st Stanza of *Lovely Peach Blossoms*, *Odes of Zhou, Classic of Poetry*

【Commentary】

The poem aims to give newlyweds congratulations. It has three stanzas. The lovely peach blossoms are used as affective images to show the beauty of the bride. The following two stanzas draw an analogy between peach trees full of fruits and numerous children the bride will give birth to. As the ancients believed that "the more children, the happier and more prosperous a family will be", the poem sings highly of the bride from the perspective of her strong fertility.

4. 汉广

【原文】

南有乔木，不可休思。汉有游女，不可求思。汉之广矣，不可泳思。江之永矣，不可方思。

《诗经·周南·汉广》首章

【释文】

南方有高大的树木，但树荫太少不适合歇息。有个女子在汉水边行走，我想追求她却感觉没有希望。这就好比汉水太宽广，不能游到对岸。好比悠长的长江水，划着小船都难以渡过。

【解析】

这是一个青年男子爱慕女子而不能得的诗歌。诗共三章。诗以高树不能休息起兴，比喻汉女虽美却不能相求的伤感。眼前的汉水因其阔广深永而不能横渡，暗示了现实中的种种阻隔，使人们无法实现愿望。

4.The Broad Han River

There are tall trees in the south, but they are not luxuriant to cool people. The girl is walking along the Han River. Though I want to court her, I'm afraid I will end up in vain. It's like the broad Han River that one cannot swim across it. It's like the wide Yangtze River that one cannot row across it.

From the 1st Stanza of *The Broad Han River*,
Odes of Zhou, Classic of Poetry

【Commentary】

The poem is about the young man who loves a girl but cannot win her heart. It has three stanzas. The poem uses tall trees that are not luxuriant to cool people in the 1st stanza as affective images to show the sadness of the young man who cannot win the love of the beautiful girl. The Han River that is too broad to cross implies barriers in the real life that keep people from achieving their aspirations.

詩經選譯

汝坟

Levees of Ru River

5. 汝坟

【原文】

鲂鱼赪尾，王室如毁。虽则如毁，父母孔迩。

《诗经·周南·汝坟》三章

【释文】

鲂鱼的尾巴因为疲劳而变成红色，官府的暴政急如烈火燃烧。虽然暴政像烈火烧，但父母很近却不能忘记。

【解析】

这是一首女子思念丈夫的诗歌。诗共三章。这里写妻子能体谅丈夫因为暴虐的王政而奔波在外的现实，但仍然希望丈夫要想到家中还有父母需要赡养，不要忘记为父母尽孝的责任，这是委婉地表达了对丈夫早日回家的期待。

5.Levees of Ru River

The tail of a gurnard turns red when it's exhausted. The tyrannies of the ruler are like raging blazes. Although the tyrannies of the ruler are like raging blazes, we cannot forget our parents who live nearby.

From the 3rd Stanza of *Levees of Ru River,*
Odes of Zhou, Classic of Poetry

【Commentary】

The poem is about the wife who misses her husband. It has three stanzas. The wife is aware of the fact that her husband has to run errands due to the tyrannies of the ruler, but she hopes that her husband will not neglect his filial duty. By saying so, the wife euphemistically expresses her wish to see her husband come home at an early date.

6. 草虫

【原文】

喓喓草虫，趯趯阜螽。未见君子，忧心忡忡。亦既见止，亦既觏止，我心则降。

《诗经·召南·草虫》首章

【释文】

秋天的蝈蝈喓喓地鸣叫，蚱蜢也蹦蹦跳跳。很久没有见到我的夫君，我担心又忧愁。倘若我们已经相见了，也已经团聚了，我也就放心了。

【解析】

这是一首思妇诗歌。诗共三章。诗歌通过描写物候的变化来表达夫妻离别之苦。诗以蝈蝈的鸣叫和蚱蜢的蹦跳起兴，预示秋天的到来，也暗示着离别已近一年的时间。诗中还设想到这个女子与丈夫未见之前的忧愁、相见后的喜悦。前后心情的变化正是相思太深的表现。

6.Katydids

Katydids chirp in autumn. Grasshoppers leap vigorously. I was worried and distressed that I had not seen my husband for quite a long time. But if we were reunited, I would be relieved.

From the 1st Stanza of *Katydids*,
Odes of Shao, Classic of Poetry

【Commentary】

The poem is about the wife who misses her husband. It has three stanzas. The change of season indicates the pain of separation between the husband and the wife. Chirps of katydids and leaps of grasshoppers at the beginning of the poem are used as affective images to indicate the arrival of autumn and the nearly one-year separation between the wife and her husband. The wife is distressed before seeing her husband but joyful after seeing him. Her change of moods reflects that she misses her husband dreadfully.

7. 行露

【原文】

谁谓雀无角，何以穿我屋？谁谓女无家，何以速我狱？虽速我狱，室家不足。

《诗经·召南·行露》二章

【释文】

谁说雀儿没有嘴，那它凭什么啄穿我的屋子？谁说你没有老婆，你凭什么逼我坐牢？就算你逼我坐了牢房，但你的逼婚理由实在太荒唐。

【解析】

这是一首写女子拒婚的诗歌。诗共有三章。诗中写一个有妻室的男子先是用花言巧语骗婚，接着又以打官司的方式来威胁，但这个女子保持清醒的头脑，面对威逼利诱，毫不犹豫拒绝了。

7.Roadside Dew

Who says finches have no beaks? If so, how can they peck my house? Who says you have no wives? What claim do you have to send me to prison? Even if you imprison me by force, your excuses to force me to marry you are too absurd.

From the 2nd Stanza of *Roadside Dew*,
Odes of Shao, Classic of Poetry

【Commentary】

The poem is about the young woman who refuses to marry. It has three stanzas. The poem depicts the married man who first tries to coax the girl to marry him and then threatens to go to court. The girl is sober-minded in front of the carrot and stick and refuses the man without hesitation.

詩經選譯

摽有梅
Withered Plums

8．摽有梅

【原文】

摽有梅，其实七兮。求我庶士，迨其吉兮。

《诗经·召南·摽有梅》首章

【释文】

梅子虽然渐渐地凋落了，但枝头上还剩下大部分的果实。追求我的年青人，你要趁着吉日赶紧来娶我。

【解析】

这是一首写女子待嫁的诗歌。诗共三章。诗歌先写梅子开始凋落，暗示女子已经到了结婚的年龄，希望年青男子能够选择好日子来求婚。先秦时期，男子三十岁未娶、女子二十岁未嫁，在仲春月会上，都可以自由选择对象，不必举行正式的婚礼就可以同居。这首诗反映的应该就是这种情况。

8.Withered Plums

Plums are withering, but many are still hanging on trees. My love, please select an auspicious day as soon as possible to marry me.

From the 1st Stanza of *Withered Plums*,

Odes of Shao, Classic of Poetry

【Commentary】

The poem is about the young woman who is to get married. It has three stanzas. The poem starts with the withered plums, implying that the woman who is at the marriage age hopes her love to propose marriage. In the pre-Qin period, single men at 30 and single women at 20 were allowed to choose their loves at the mid-spring festival and cohabit without having wedding ceremonies. The scenario was described in the poem.

9. 江有汜

【原文】

江有汜，之子归，不我以。不我以，其后也悔。

《诗经·召南·江有汜》首章

【释文】

长江水有支流，你的新娘也娶到了家中，你已经不需要我了。但你今天抛弃了我，将来你要后悔。

【解析】

这是一首弃妇诗。诗共三章。从诗中描绘的情形看，女主人公可能是一位商人妇。商人娶了新妇之后就抛弃了旧妻。而女主人公似乎还在期待这个商人回心转意。商业在中国先秦时代本就是末业，商人的社会地位也相对卑下。商人时常离家背井、奔走经商，因此，商人妇与其他妇女相较又有更多不幸。

9.Tributaries of the Yangtze River

The Yangtze River has its tributaries. With your newly married bride at home, you do not need me any longer. But you will regret abandoning me someday.

From the 1st Stanza of *Tributaries of the Yangtze River*, *Odes of Shao, Classic of Poetry*

【Commentary】

The poem is about an abandoned woman. It has three stanzas. From what the poem describes, the heroine is likely to be the wife of a merchant. She is abandoned after the merchant marries another woman. The heroine seems to expect her husband to change his mind. Commerce was regarded as the lowest ranking industry in the pre-Qin period and merchants had low social position. They had to do business far away from home and their wives suffered more misfortunes than wives of those who engaged in other trades.

詩經選譯

野有死麕

A Dead Roe Deer in the Wilderness

10. 野有死麕

【原文】

野有死麕，白茅包之。有女怀春，吉士诱之。

《诗经·召南·野有死麕》首章

【释文】

野地有只死獐鹿，被猎人用白色茅草包裹着。那位姑娘情窦初开，而那个青年猎人也主动上前搭讪。

【解析】

这是青年男女恋爱的诗歌。诗共三章。写这位青年猎人用他狩猎得来的獐鹿作为礼物来追求少女。从诗中所写情形看，这对青年男女应是初次相见，所以诗中用了一个“诱”字来写男子主动搭讪。诗歌后两章就写到了他们情投意合、最终在一起的情况。

10.A Dead Roe Deer in the Wilderness

There's a dead roe deer in the wilderness and it's wrapped by white couch grass by its hunter. The maiden dreams about love. The young hunter strikes up a conversation with her.

From the 1st Stanza of *A Dead Roe Deer in the Wilderness*,
Odes of Shao, Classic of Poetry

【Commentary】

The poem describes love between young people. It has three stanzas. It's about the young hunter who pursues the girl by giving her the roe deer that he has hunted as a present. The poem suggests that it's the first time for the young man and woman to see each other, so the young man strikes up a conversation with her. They fall in love with each other and decide to get married in the following two stanzas.

11. 柏舟

【原文】

我心匪石，不可转也。我心匪席，不可卷也。威仪棣棣，不可选也。

《诗经·邶风·柏舟》三章

【释文】

我的心不是一块石头，不能随便移动。我的心不是一条席子，不可任意翻卷。我的仪容娴雅，不可任人欺负。

【解析】

这是一位妇女感觉被众妾所侮的怨诗。诗共五章。这里分别用石头、席子作比喻，说明她是一个仪容娴雅、品行端正的妇女。石头可以随便移动，席子可以任意翻卷，暗示了众妾反复无常的性格。本诗是较早揭示妻妾矛盾问题的篇章。

11.A Boat of Cypress Wood

My heart is not a stone, so it cannot be moved willfully. My heart is not a mat, so it cannot be rolled up arbitrarily. I'm dignified and I will not allow others to take the liberty of bullying me.

From the 3rd Stanza of *A Boat of Cypress Wood*,
Odes of Bei, *Classic of Poetry*

【Commentary】

The poem is about the wife who is bullied by her husband's concubines. It has five stanzas. She displays her elegance, dignity and good conduct using the analogy of stones and mats. Concubines are changeable, just like stones that can be moved willfully and mats that can be rolled up arbitrarily. The poem is one of the earliest to display the conflicts between wife and concubines.

詩經選譯

绿衣
The Green Garment

12. 绿衣

【原文】

絺兮绤兮，凄其以风。我思古人，实获我心。

《诗经·邶风·绿衣》四章

【释文】

粗葛布啊细葛布，穿在身上凉爽又舒服。我想念亡故的妻子，她做的每件事都让我称心如意。

【解析】

这是一首怀念亡故妻子的诗。诗共四章。诗人看到亡妻所做的葛布衣服，觉得妻子的所作所为最能符合自己的心意，因而重新陷入悲痛之中。这种睹物思人的写法，是悼亡怀旧诗中最常见的构思，因此也成为后代这类诗歌的写作典范。

12.The Green Garment

Clothes made of ko-hemp, coarse or fine, I find them cool and comfortable on me. I miss my diseased wife. Everything she did was to my liking.

From the 4th Stanza of *The Green Garment*,

Odes of Bei, *Classic of Poetry*

【Commentary】

The poem is about the widower who misses his dead wife. It has four stanzas. The ko-hemp clothes remind the widower of his dead wife. Thinking that all she did was to his liking, the widower is plunged into sadness. It's a common style of writing in poems of its kind to associate objects with the person missed by others. The poem is a model for its kind in the later generations.

13．燕燕

【原文】

燕燕于飞，差池其羽。之子于归，远送于野。瞻望弗及，泣涕如雨！

《诗经·邶风·燕燕》首章

【释文】

一对燕子展翅飞上天，参差舒展它的翅膀。这个姑娘要出嫁了，大家远远地送到郊外。看着她渐渐消失的背影，眼泪如雨一般掉下来！

【解析】

这是一首送女子出嫁的诗歌。诗共四章。诗歌先以燕子展翅高飞来比喻女子准备远嫁。接着写远送到野外，表达了依依不舍之情。诗末写到诗人看不到离别的背影时，泪如雨下，尤其见出送别的悲伤，把抽象的离别之情写得具体而形象。

13.Swallows

A pair of swallows spreads their wings and flies high. The girl is leaving home to marry into a family far way. We escort her to as far as the outskirts. Her back has been gradually blurred, and our tears stream down our faces.

From the 1st Stanza of *Swallows*,
Odes of Bei, *Classic of Poetry*

【Commentary】

The poem is about the girl who is going to marry far away. It has four stanzas. The poem depicts the girl who is going to marry far away using the analogy of swallows flying high in the sky. Her family escort her to as far as the outskirts and feel reluctant to bid farewell. At the end of the poem, her family burst into tears watching her blurred back. Sadness of bidding farewell is depicted in this way. The poem describes such grief in a vivid way.

詩經選譯

击鼓

Beating Drums

14. 击鼓

【原文】

死生契阔，与子成说。执子之手，与子偕老。

《诗经·邶风·击鼓》四章

【释文】

生死永远都不会分离，这是我和你立下的誓言。紧紧握住你的手，和你一起生活到老。

【解析】

这是卫国的戍卒思归不得的诗。诗共五章。这一章是诗人回忆在家时与爱人在一起时发下的誓言。他们曾经发誓要同生共死，白头偕老。但现在他在外服兵役，不知何时才能回家；且在战场上，生死难卜，曾经立下的誓言当然也难以实现了。

14.Beating Drums

Even death cannot separate you and me. It's my oath to you. Tightly holding your hands, I will live with you till the end of my day.

From the 4th Stanza of *Beating Drums*,
Odes of Bei, *Classic of Poetry*

【Commentary】

The poem is about the garrison solider who misses home, but cannot return home. It has five stanzas. In the quoted stanza, the hero recalls the oath he swears to his wife. He has promised to live with his wife till the end of his day, but he is on campaign and does not know when he can return home. Even worse, he is faced with the threat of death at the battlefield. It's very difficult for him to honor his commitment.

15. 凯风

【原文】

凯风自南，吹彼棘心。棘心夭夭，母氏劬劳。

《诗经·邶风·凯风》首章

【释文】

南方吹来温暖的和风，吹拂着酸枣树的嫩芽。酸枣树长得又嫩又壮，母亲实在很辛劳。

【解析】

这是一首儿子歌颂母亲并作自责的诗。诗共四章。诗歌用凯风吹拂酸枣的嫩芽来比喻母亲抚养七个儿子的辛劳。诗歌后三章写到儿子们的愧疚，自责不能慰悦母亲。中国古代重视孝道，父母抚养之恩深如海、重如山。儿女的孝敬不仅仅体现在对父母的物质供养上，更重要的是在精神上使父母得到愉悦。

15.Warm Breeze

Warm breeze from the south blows the twigs of wild jujube trees. They grow well. My mother is toil-worn.

From the 1st Stanza of *Warm Breeze*,
Odes of Bei, *Classic of Poetry*

【Commentary】

The poem is about the son who sings highly of his mother and blames himself. It has four stanzas. The poem depicts the hard work of raising seven sons using the analogy of warm breeze that blows the twigs of wild jujube trees. In the following three stanzas, the sons blame themselves for not being able to please their mother. The ancients attached great importance to filial piety. Children should be deeply indebted to their parents for their parenting. Filial piety is fulfilled not only by providing material support to one's parents, but also by making them happy.

16. 泉水

【原文】

毖彼泉水，亦流于淇。有怀于卫，靡日不思。娈彼诸姬，聊与之谋。

《诗经·邶风·泉水》首章

【释文】

泉水涓涓地流淌，一直流到了淇水。我心里想着我的故乡卫国，没有一天能忘记。陪嫁的姊妹们都美丽贤惠，我姑且与她们商议吧。

【解析】

这是一首嫁到别国的卫女思归不得的诗。诗共四章。先秦时期，女子出嫁之后，是不能轻易回娘家的。卫女远嫁别国，背离故土，她思念家乡的心情很迫切，只能与陪嫁的姑娘商量对策。

16.Spring Water

Spring water trickles into the Qi River. I miss my hometown the State of Wei and I have never forgotten my hometown for a moment. My maidservants who have come with me from my hometown to my husband's home are beautiful and nice, so I will talk about my feelings of homesickness with them.

From the 1st Stanza of *Spring Water*,
Odes of Bei, *Classic of Poetry*

【Commentary】

The poem describes the girl of the State of Wei who has married into the family of another state. The Wei girl misses her hometown, but cannot go back. It has four stanzas. In the pre-Qin period, married women could not go back to their parents' home at will. The Wei girl marries into the family of another state and lives far away from home. She is desperately homesick, but the only thing she can do is to talk about her feelings of homesickness with her maidservants.

詩經選譯

北风

North Wind

17. 北风

【原文】

北风其凉，雨雪其雱。惠而好我，携手同行。其虚其邪？既亟只且！

《诗经·邶风·北风》首章

【释文】

北风冷冽，大雪纷飞。同甘共苦的伙伴们，我们一起携手逃难吧。为什么还要犹豫徘徊呢？赶紧离开这个危险的地方吧！

【解析】

这是卫国人民不堪暴政、相约逃亡的诗。诗共三章。中国诗教崇尚温柔敦厚，要求情感表达含蓄平和。但对暴政的舍弃斥责，人们在抒发愤怒的情感时也表现得非常大胆，这是人们对统治者的怨愤，所谓“乱世之音怨以怒”。

17.North Wind

The north wind chills our skin and snow falls heavily. My friends, you have been through thick and thin with me, please flee with me. Why are you hesitating? Let's flee from the dangerous place.

From the 1st Stanza of *North Wind*,

Odes of Bei, *Classic of Poetry*

【Commentary】

The poem is about people of the State of Wei who wanted to flee together for the tyrannies of the ruler were beyond endurance. It has three stanzas. Chinese poems value modesty in expressing feelings, but poets are boldly explicit in expressing their anger against tyrannical rulers. The saying goes that music is full of resentment in the chaotic times.

詩經選譯

新台

The New Terrace

18. 新台

【原文】

新台有泚，河水弥弥。燕婉之求，籧篨不鲜。

《诗经·邶风·新台》首章

【释文】

新台辉煌敞亮，黄河流水洋洋而过。本想嫁一个如意的夫婿，却没想到嫁了个癞蛤蟆一样的丑男人。

【解析】

这是卫人讽刺卫宣公劫夺儿媳的诗。诗共三章。卫宣公与后母乱伦，又劫夺儿媳，都是荒诞无耻的行为，不合于礼仪，所以被人们憎恨挖苦。

18. The New Terrace

The new terrace is splendid. The Yellow River flows along it. I want to marry the man I love, but what I marry is a man as ugly as a toad.

From the 1st Stanza of *The New Terrace*,
Odes of Bei, *Classic of Poetry*

【Commentary】

The poem satirizes Duke Xuan of Wei who took his daughter-in-law as his wife by force. Duke Xuan of Wei first committed incest with his step mother and later forcibly took his daughter-in-law as his wife. What he did was shameless and corrupted public morals, so he was satirized by his people.

19. 墙有茨

【原文】

墙有茨，不可埽也。中冓之言，不可道也。所可道也？言之丑也。

《诗经·鄘风·墙有茨》首章

【释文】

墙上长有蒺藜草，这草是扫除不了的。宫廷的秘密传言，不可对外乱说。如果对外乱说呢？这些丑闻肯定让人觉得羞耻。

【解析】

这是一首揭露卫国统治者淫乱无耻的诗歌。诗共三章。以墙上的蒺藜无法扫除起兴，说明卫国人民对这种败坏人伦的秽行深恶痛绝。

19.Sandbur on the Wall

There's sandbur on the wall, which cannot be eradicated. There are rumors about the court, which cannot be spread. If the rumors are spread, what consequences will ensue? People will feel ashamed of those who are involved in the scandals.

From the 1st Stanza of *Sandbur on the Wall*,
Odes of Yong, *Classic of Poetry*

【Commentary】

The poem reveals the licentious and unashamed rulers of the State of Wei. It has three stanzas. The sandbur on the wall that cannot be eradicated is used as an affective image to show that Wei people abhorred the scandalous conduct.

詩經選譯

相鼠

Rats

20. 相鼠

【原文】

相鼠有皮，人而无仪。人而无仪，不死何为？

《诗经·鄘风·相鼠》首章

【释文】

老鼠尚且有皮，人却没有严肃端庄的威仪。人没有威仪，为何还不去死？

【解析】

这是一首讽刺统治者无礼仪的诗。诗共三章。在周代，统治者已经制订了一套严密的礼仪来规范人们的行为，上至统治者，下至平民百姓都要遵守，以维护统治的秩序。但统治者因为权力过大、没有监管，往往违背这些礼节而为所欲为。诗歌以老鼠尚且有皮来起兴，指斥这些统治者虚伪无耻。

20.Rats

Rats have their skin, but humanity has no dignified demeanor. Why the man without dignified demeanor does not commit suicide?

From the 1st Stanza of *Rats*,

Odes of Yong, *Classic of Poetry*

【Commentary】

The poem satirizes rulers who ignore rites. It has three stanzas. Rulers of the Zhou Dynasty established strict rules concerning rites to maintain their reigning order. All the people, including rulers and commoners should observe them. However, some rulers ignored the rules and acted willfully as they had absolute power. The poem uses rats that have skin as affective images to rebuke the rulers for being hypocritical and shameless.

21. 载驰

【原文】

我行其野，芃芃其麦。控于大邦，谁因谁极？大夫君子，无我有尤。百尔所思，不如我所之。

《诗经·鄘风·载驰》五章

【释文】

我走在卫国郊外的田野上，麦子茂盛地生长。想要到大国去陈诉，但又有哪个国家可以为我们排忧解难呢？许国的当权者，不要指责我的过错。你们设想的种种方案，都不如我亲自前往慰问一趟。

【解析】

这是描写许穆夫人回漕吊唁卫侯的诗。诗共五章。公元前660年，狄人入侵卫国。因卫懿公好鹤而不恤国民，所以卫国被狄人占领。宋桓公把卫国难民接过黄河，并安置在漕邑。出嫁于许国的许穆夫人心急如焚，星夜兼程赶到漕邑吊唁，在途中写下了这首诗，表现了强烈的爱国主义精神。

21.Gallop

Passing through the fields in the suburbs of the State of Wei, I notice wheat is growing well. I want to seek help from big states, but which state can solve our problems? Rulers of the State of Xu, please do not criticize me for what I'm doing. All your solutions are dwarfed by my condolence visit.

From the 5th Stanza of *Gallop*,
Odes of Yong, *Classic of Poetry*

【Commentary】

The poem is about Madam Xu Mu who paid a condolence visit to Cao to mourn the death of the duke of Wei. It has five stanzas. The State of Wei was invaded in 660 B.C. As the main concern of Duke Yi of Wei was cranes rather than his people, his state was occupied by the invaders. Duke Huan of Song had the Wei refugees fetched to the other side of the Yellow River and had them settled in Cao. Madam Xu Mu who had married to the State of Xu was desperately anxious and travelled day and night without stopping to pay a condolence visit to Cao. On her way to Cao, she wrote the poem, showing her intense patriotism.

詩經選譯

考槃

Build a Wooden House

22. 考槃

【原文】

考槃在涧，硕人之宽。独寐寤言，永矢弗谖。

《诗经·卫风·考槃》首章

【释文】

在山涧建一间木屋来居住，贤人觉得舒畅宽慰。就算是一个人独自生活，也永远不会违背隐居的高洁理想。

【解析】

这是一首描写隐居独善其身的诗歌。诗共三章。写诗人住在自造的木屋里，隐居到山涧之畔，远离喧嚷，虽然只是独自一人，但自得其乐。中国传统文化对隐居不仕、洁身谨独的行为一向赞美有加，认为他们保有赤子至诚、天真纯朴的心，这首诗也是最早表现这种文化的诗歌。

22.Build a Wooden House

Build a wooden house by mountain streams and a man of virtue feels refreshed and comfortable living in such a wooden house. Even if he lives alone, he will not abandon his noble ideals.

From the 1st Stanza of *Build a Wooden House*,
Odes of Wei, *Classic of Poetry*

【Commentary】

The poem is about those who live in seclusion to maintain their integrity. It has three stanzas. The poet lived in a self-built wooden house and enjoyed living alone by mountain streams, separating him from the crowds. Traditional Chinese culture sung highly of those who would rather maintain their integrity by being recluses than work for the sovereign. They were highly commended for retaining their integrity. The poem is one of the earliest to show the culture.

23. 硕人

【原文】

手如柔荑，肤如凝脂。领如蝤蛴，齿如瓠犀。螓首蛾眉，巧笑倩兮，美目盼兮。

《诗经·卫风·硕人》二章

【释文】

手指如嫩荑柔嫩，皮肤如凝脂白润。颈项如蝤蛴洁白，牙齿如瓠子洁白整齐。额头方正蛾眉弯细，笑时两颊现出酒窝，望时眼睛黑白分明。

【解析】

这是卫人赞美卫庄公夫人齐庄姜的诗歌。诗共四章。用六个比喻，从手、皮肤、颈、齿、额、笑容、眼睛等方面赞美庄姜。这是中国古代诗歌中，从正面细腻刻画女子美貌的最早诗篇。

23.The Tall and Beautiful Lady

Her fingers are as tender as sprouts. Her skin is as white and smooth as congealed lard. Her neck is as white as longicorn's larva. Her teeth are as even as seeds of bottle gourds. Her forehead is square and her eyebrows are thin and curved. When she smiles, she has two dimples in her cheeks. When she looks around, her eyes are dark and bright.

From the 2nd Stanza of *The Tall and Beautiful Lady*,
Odes of Wei, *Classic of Poetry*

【Commentary】

The poem eulogizes Qi Zhuangjiang, the wife of Duke Zhuang of Wei. It has four stanzas. With six similes, the poem eulogizes about her fingers, skin, neck, teeth, forehead, smile and eyes. It's the earliest poem to describe the beauty of a girl in detail.

詩經選譯

氓

Mr. Wrong

24. 氓

【原文】

桑之未落，其叶沃若。于嗟鸠兮，无食桑葚。于嗟女兮，无与士耽。士之耽兮，犹可说也。女之耽兮，不可说也。

《诗经·卫风·氓》三章

【释文】

桑叶未凋落之前，叶子丰满润泽。斑鸠鸟啊，千万不要贪吃桑葚。年轻的姑娘啊，千万不要迷恋男子。男子若是爱上你，尚可解脱。女子要是爱上男子，就难以解脱了。

【解析】

这是一首弃妇诗。诗共六章。很早以前，中国人就懂得种桑养蚕织布，男耕女织，所以，诗歌以桑起兴。此处以桑叶没有凋落之前的丰满润泽来比喻自己曾经的年轻貌美，并以此告诫年轻女子不要与无德的男子胡缠，以免陷入痛苦和悔恨之中，表现了弃妇刚强的性格和反抗的精神。

24.Mr. Wrong

Mulberry leaves are luxuriant before withering and falling. Turtledoves, do not be greedy for mulberries. Young girls, do not be obsessed with men. If men fall in love with you, they can easily forget you. If girls fall in love with men, it'll be difficult to free them from the pain of love.

From the 3rd Stanza of *Mr. Wrong*,

Odes of Wei, *Classic of Poetry*

[Commentary]

The poem is about an abandoned woman. It has six stanzas. Chinese people started growing mulberry trees for silkworm breeding and weaving a long time ago. Men tilled the land while women weaved. So the poem uses mulberry leaves as affective images to draw an analogy between luxuriant mulberry leaves and the lady when she is young and pretty and warns young women not to show interest in men with no virtues so as to avoid deep sorrow and rue. It shows that the abandoned woman is of strong character and spirit of resistance.

25. 竹竿

【原文】

泉源在左，淇水在右。女子有行，远兄弟父母。

《诗经·卫风·竹竿》二章

【释文】

泉源在左边，淇水在右边。姑娘出嫁到别国，远离父母和兄弟。

【解析】

这是一位卫国女子出嫁别国、思念家乡的诗。诗共四章。中国古代，女子出嫁到别的诸侯国之后，除非被休或夫家所在的国家灭亡了，才能回到父母之国。女子出嫁之后，有可能一辈子都见不到自己的父母兄弟了，因此，她们的思乡心情非常沉重。

25. Bamboo Poles

The source of water is on the left while the Qi River is on the right. The girl is going to marry to another country, far away from her parents and brothers.

From the 2nd Stanza of *Bamboo Poles*,
Odes of Wei, *Classic of Poetry*

【Commentary】

The poem is about the girl of Wei who marries to another country and misses her family and hometown. It has four stanzas. In ancient China, women who married into other vassal states could not return to their motherland unless being divorced by their husbands or their husbands' countries perished. It's possible that married women could not see her parents and brothers for the rest of their life, so they were desperately homesick.

詩經選譯

河广

The Broad Yellow River

26. 河广

【原文】

谁谓河广？一苇杭之。谁谓宋远？跂予望之。

《诗经·卫风·河广》首章

【释文】

谁说黄河很宽广？一叶小舟就可以横渡了。谁说宋国很遥远？踮起脚跟就能望到。

【解析】

这是一位住在卫国的宋人思归不得的诗歌。诗共两章。宋、卫两国以黄河相隔，一水相望。本来路途并不遥远，但宋人却因种种原因不能回到故国，因此有此感慨。一叶小舟就可以横渡的黄河，踮起脚跟就能望到的故国，都说明在空间上很近，但返回故国又是如此的艰难。在这种对比反衬中，诗人寄寓他国的痛苦就显得更深沉了。

26.The Broad Yellow River

Who says the Yellow River is broad? You can cross the river by rowing a small boat. Who says the State of Song is far away? You can see it by standing on your heels.

From the 1st Stanza of *The Broad Yellow River*,
Odes of Wei, *Classic of Poetry*

【Commentary】

The poem is about the man of Song living in the State of Wei who misses his hometown but cannot return. It has two stanzas. The State of Song and the State of Wei were separated by the Yellow River. Although they were not far away, the man of Song could not return to his hometown due to several reasons, so he was deeply distressed. The two countries were close, so one could cross the Yellow River by rowing a small boat and see his motherland by standing on his heels. However, it was very difficult for the poet to return home. The poet showed his great distress by making the sharp contrast.

27. 伯兮

【原文】

自伯之东，首如飞蓬。岂无膏沐？谁适为容！

《诗经·卫风·伯兮》二章

【释文】

自从丈夫去东征后，我在家里蓬头垢面。难道没有洗发油？只是我修饰容貌是为了取悦谁呢！

【解析】

这是女子思念远征的丈夫的诗歌。诗共四章。写丈夫出征之后，女子在家无心修饰容颜的情形。诗歌并不直接叙写女子对丈夫的思念，而是写她在家中蓬头垢面的样子，反而衬出这个女子对丈夫深沉的爱意和思念之情。中国有一句古话，说“女为悦己者容”，意思就是讲女子的梳妆打扮是给欣赏自己容颜的心上人看的。而今这个女子的丈夫远征不归，她当然无心修饰容颜了。

27.My Husband

I'm unkempt since my husband has been on an expedition eastward. Is it because I have no shampoo? No. Who am I going to please if I'm well-grooomed?

From the 2nd Stanza of *My Husband*,
Odes of Wei, *Classic of Poetry*

【Commentary】

The poem is about the woman who misses her husband who has been on a military expedition. It has four stanzas. The quoted stanza is about the woman who is unkempt after her husband has been on an expedition. The poem does not directly describe how the wife misses her husband. By depicting the wife with unkempt appearance, the poem shows how deeply the wife loves and misses her husband. A Chinese saying goes that women doll themselves up to please the men they love. As her husband is on an expedition, she's in no mood for grooming.

詩經選譯

木瓜
Papayas

28. 木瓜

【原文】

投我以木瓜，报之以琼琚。匪报也，永以为好也。

《诗经·卫风·木瓜》首章

【释文】

她赠送我一个木瓜，我回送她一块美玉。不仅仅是报答她，而是以此表示我们永远相爱。

【解析】

这是一首男女互送定情礼物的诗歌。诗共三章。中国是一个礼仪之邦，待人接物都遵照一定礼节。在古代中国，无论男女都喜欢在衣带上挂装饰物，此种装饰物以玉为贵，称为玉佩。男女相好之后，男子往往赠送爱人玉佩作为定情信物。

28.Papayas

She gave me a papaya and I gave her a piece of jade in return. It's not a token of appreciation, but a token of love.

From the 1st Stanza of *Papayas*,

Odes of Wei, *Classic of Poetry*

【Commentary】

The poem is about a pair of young couple who gives each other gifts as a token of love. It has three stanzas. China is a state of ceremonies, so rites should be observed in dealing with people. Ancient Chinese men and women liked to wear ornaments and the most precious ornaments were jade pendants, so men liked to give the girls they adored jade pendants as a token of love.

29. 黍离

【原文】

彼黍离离，彼稷之苗。行迈靡靡，中心摇摇。知我者，谓我心忧；不知我者，谓我何求。悠悠苍天，此何人哉！

《诗经 · 王风 · 黍离》首章

【释文】

糜子生长茂盛，高粱苗绿油油。我慢慢地走在长路上，心里却愁闷得难受。了解我的人说我心烦忧，不了解我的人说我有所求。高高在上的老天爷啊，是谁害得我们流离失所啊！

【解析】

这是诗人抒发迁都时难舍故旧家园的诗歌。诗共三章。西周的首都本来是在镐京的，但西周末年的幽王无道，导致国家灭亡，周平王把都城迁到了洛邑（今洛阳）。诗人经过镐京时，看到旧都城一片荒凉破败，写下了这首诗。诗人在迁徙的路上，看到处处是青葱翠绿的庄稼，心中却充满了忧伤。诗人背井离乡的无奈无人能知，甚至被误解。诗歌开头写一派生机盎然的景象，与诗人离乡的忧伤相衬，正是中国古人所说的“以乐景写哀情，其情更哀”之意。

29.Lush Broom Corn Millet Crops

Broom corn millet crops are lush and sorghum leaves are green. Walking slowly on a long road, I feel very upset. Those who understand me say I'm worried while those who don't understand me say I aspire to something. Oh, Heaven, who has forced us to be displaced?

From the 1st Stanza of *Lush Broom Corn Millet Crops, Odes of Wang, Classic of Poetry*

【Commentary】

The poet expressed his reluctance to abandon his home when the capital had to be moved. It has three stanzas. The capital of Western Zhou was initially at Haojing. King You, the last ruler of Western Zhou was incompetent and cruel, so the Western Zhou Dynasty was destructed. King Ping of Eastern Zhou moved the capital to Luoyi (the current Luoyang). The poet wrote the poem when he witnessed a scene of desolation of Haojing, the old capital. On his way to the new capital, the poet saw lush crops, but he felt distressed. He was forced to leave his hometown, but few could understand his feelings and some even misunderstood him. The scene of vitality was in sharp contrast with the distress of the poet who was forced to leave his hometown. The ancients believed that grief was on full display when described with happy scenes.

詩經選譯

君子于役

My Husband Is Fulfilling His Corvee Duties at a Remote Place

30. 君子于役

【原文】

君子于役，不知其期。曷至哉？鸡栖于埘。日之夕矣，羊牛下来。君子于役，如之何勿思！

《诗经·王风·君子于役》首章

【释文】

丈夫到远方去服役，不知服役的期限。什么时候才能回家啊？鸡都已经飞回墙上的鸡窝了。傍晚的太阳也下山了，牛羊也从山坡上回栏了。丈夫还在远方服役，这叫我怎么不思念呢！

【解析】

这是一位妇女思念她服役于外的丈夫的诗歌。诗共两章。诗歌写丈夫服徭役归期无限，妻子思念不已，尤其见到傍晚归巢的鸡儿和从山上归来的牛羊，这种思念就更加强烈了。诗中不直接写妻子的思念，而是选择了一个傍晚家禽、家畜回家的细节来表达情感。中国很重视家庭的团聚，日出而作，日落而息，不管白天去到哪里，晚上一定回到家中。诗中女子也是这样一种心态，因此，日薄西山时，她又燃起了与家人团聚的希望。

30.My Husband Is Fulfilling His Corvee Duties at a Remote Place

My husband is fulfilling his corvee duties at a remote place. I don't know when he can be relieved of the duties? When will he come back? Chickens have flied back to their coop on the wall. The sun has gone down and cows and goats have returned to their barns on the slope. But my husband is fulfilling his corvee duties at a remote place. How can I stop missing him?

From the 1st Stanza of *My Husband Is Fulfilling His Corvee Duties at a Remote Place*, *Odes of Wang*, *Classic of Poetry*

【Commentary】

The poem is about the wife who misses her husband who is fulfilling his corvee duties at a remote place. It has two stanzas. The husband has to fulfill his corvee duties for an indefinite time limit, so the wife misses her husband dreadfully. Such feelings become stronger when she sees chickens, cows and goats come back at sunset. The poet does not directly describe how the wife misses her husband. Instead, the poet uses the chickens, cows and goats that come back at sunset to express the feelings of the wife. Chinese people attach great importance to family reunion. They go out to work in the morning and come back home in the evening. No matter where they go in the daytime, they are expected to return home at night. The lady in the poem thinks likewise. So the sunset has rekindled her hope of having her husband come back.

31. 兔爰

【原文】

有兔爰爰，雉离于罗。我生之初，尚无为。我生之后，逢此百罹，尚寐无吪！

《诗经·王风·兔爰》首章

【释文】

兔子悠闲自得，野鸡却不幸落网。我小的时候，还没有军役。我长大之后，却遇上了各种各样的苦难，我只想睡觉不愿诉说了！

【解析】

这是一首伤时感事的诗。诗共三章。诗歌以兔子的悠闲和野鸡的落网起兴，说明世事之无常。接着写诗人出生之初与长大之后的迥异差别。这种对比的写法，道出了人生的巨大落差，其无奈、郁闷之情溢于言表。这诗大约写于西周末东周初，易代之际，国家动荡不安，人民也遭受流离迁徙之苦。

31.A Free Rabbit

The rabbit is free while the pheasant is unfortunately caught. When I was young, there was no military service. Nevertheless, after I grow up, I have to endure the immense amount of sufferings. I don't want to talk more about my misery. I want nothing but sleep.

From the 1st Stanza of *A Free Rabbit*,

Odes of Wang, *Classic of Poetry*

【Commentary】

The poet depicted his great sorrow at the current situation. It has three stanzas. By using the free rabbit and the caught pheasant as affective images in the beginning, the poet showed the unpredictability of human life. Then the poet contrasted the old days when he was young with the days after he grew up to show the huge difference. From the words, readers can easily understand the helplessness and sorrow of the poet. The poem was written around the end of Western Zhou and the beginning of Eastern Zhou when the state was in turbulence and people suffered displacement.

詩經選譯

采葛
Pick Kudzu Vines

32. 采葛

【原文】

彼采萧兮，一日不见，如三秋兮。

《诗经·王风·采葛》二章

【释文】

那个姑娘去采艾蒿了，虽然只有一天没见到她，但我却觉得像隔了三年一样。

【解析】

这是一首思念情人的诗歌。诗共三章。这位男子非常喜欢那位勤劳的女子，心中无限爱慕。诗中通过夸张的手法，把抽象的相思之情写得很形象，一天不见，却有三年不见的感觉。此外，中国古人习惯用秋天这个收获的季节来代替一年，所以三秋就是三年。

32.Pick Kudzu Vines

The girl has gone to pick mugwort. A single day apart seems like three autumns.

From the 2nd Stanza of *Pick Kudzu Vines*,
Odes of Wang, Classic of Poetry

【Commentary】

The poem is about the man who misses his love. It has three stanzas. The man in the poem loves the diligent girl very much. The poet uses exaggeration to vividly describe the feelings of missing one's love. A single day apart seems like three autumns. Ancient Chinese liked to use autumn, the harvest season to refer to a whole year, so three autumns referred to three years.

33. 大车

【原文】

谷则异室，死则同穴。谓予不信，有如皦日！

《诗经·王风·大车》三章

【释文】

我们活着不能住一起，死后一定要埋在同一个坟墓。不要怀疑我的誓言，太阳都可以为我作证！

【解析】

这是一首女子热恋情人的诗歌。诗共三章。诗中写她很想与爱人同居，甚至对天发誓：虽然生不能同居，但死后一定要埋在一起。然而她因为不知爱人心中想法如何，所以不敢私奔。她对情人发出的誓言，显得大胆而热烈，与多数诗歌含蓄表达爱意的写法不大相同。

33. A Large Cart

If we cannot live together when alive, we will be buried in the same tomb when dead. Do not suspect my ability to keep my promise. I swear by the sun.

From the 3rd Stanza of *A Large Cart*,
Odes of Wang, *Classic of Poetry*

【Commentary】

The poem is about the girl who's madly in love. It has three stanzas. The girl wants to live with her love and swears by Heaven that even if they cannot live together when alive, they will be buried in the same tomb. She is uncertain about her love's thoughts, so she does not dare to elope. The girl is bold and ardent in expressing her love, which is strikingly different from the restrained and implicit way of expressing love in most of poems.

詩經選譯

缁衣

The Black Mandarin Costume

34. 缁衣

【原文】

缁衣之宜兮，敝，予又改为兮。适子之馆兮，还，予授子之粲兮。

《诗经·郑风·缁衣》首章

【释文】

黑色朝服真合身，破了，我给你再做一套。你先去官府忙公事，回来，我为你准备一顿美餐。

【解析】

这是一首赠衣诗。诗共三章。诗中“予”的身份，看来像是穿缁衣的人的妻妾。诗写改衣、试衣，洋溢着一种温馨的亲情。夫唱妇随是古代中国人的理想追求，这个场景正寄寓了中国人家和万事兴的期待。

34. The Black Mandarin Costume

The black mandarin costume fits you very well. I will make you a new one as it's worn. Please go to your office and do your official duty. When you come back, I will reward you with delicious food.

From the 1st Stanza of *The Black Mandarin Costume*,
Odes of Zheng, *Classic of Poetry*

【Commentary】

The poem is about giving clothes as a gift. It has three stanzas. The person who gives the clothes in the poem seems like the wife or concubine of the man who wears the black mandarin costume. The poem is full of deep familial affection by describing the scenes of having clothes altered and tried on. In the ancient Chinese' opinion, the ideal family life was that when the husband sung, the wife would accompany, conveying the idea of Chinese that the family that lives in harmony will prosper.

35. 将仲子

【原文】

将仲子兮！无逾我园，无折我树檀。岂敢爱之？畏人之多言。仲可怀也，人之多言，亦可畏也。

《诗经·郑风·将仲子》三章

【释文】

二哥你听我讲！你不要翻过我家的花园，不要折断我种的檀树。我哪里是心痛这些檀树？只是怕流言蜚语。我爱慕二哥，但是担心别人的闲话，想想心里都很害怕。

【解析】

这是女子拒绝恋人的诗歌。诗共三章。这对男女正处于热恋之中，情投意合。但这个女子心中又很矛盾，想跟情人在一起，但又害怕父母兄长的责骂以及外人的流言蜚语，所以犹豫不决。古代中国婚姻文化重视媒妁之言、父母之命，儿女虽然希望自由选择意中人，但也往往屈从父母的意愿，这又常常导致父母与儿女之间出现矛盾。

35.My Dear Second Cousin

My second cousin, please listen to me. Do not climb over the walls of my garden nor snap branches of the sandalwood trees that I planted. It's not the sandalwood trees that I feel sad about. It's the gossip I'm afraid of. I adore you, but I'm scared of gossip.

From the 3rd Stanza of *My Dear Second Cousin*,

Odes of Zheng, *Classic of Poetry*

【Commentary】

The poem is about the girl who rejects her love. It has three stanzas. The couple is in deep love with each other, but the girl is hesitant. On the one hand, she wants to stay with her love. On the other, she is afraid of scolding from her parents and siblings and gossip by others. In ancient China, words of matchmakers and dictates of parents were of paramount importance in terms of marriage. The youth may have their loved ones, but they had to yield to their parents, leading to conflicts between parents and their children.

詩經選譯

女曰鸡鸣

Roosters Crow at Dawn

36. 女曰鸡鸣

【原文】

弋言加之，与子宜之。宜言饮酒，与子偕老。琴瑟在御，莫不静好。

《诗经·郑风·女曰鸡鸣》二章

【释文】

你射中了野鸭与大雁，我为你烹调菜肴。我们品尝美酒佳肴，夫唱妇随到终老。你弹琴我鼓瑟，我们的生活美满和好。

【解析】

这是一首写新婚夫妇的诗。诗共三章。诗歌描写一对新婚夫妇情投意合、欢乐和美的家庭生活。诗末以琴瑟相和来比喻夫妻和谐，对中国传统文化影响很大，以后写夫妻关系多用琴瑟设喻。此外，古代士人读书学有所成，年轻时希望能够出来做官、建立功业。等功成名就之后，告老辞官，与家人享受天伦之乐，这是士人憧憬的生活模式。出则掌持天下，入则夫唱妇随，更是古代中国人最理想的期待。

36.Roosters Crow at Dawn

You have shot dead wild ducks and gooses, and I will cook a meal for you. Let's enjoy good wine and delicious food. Whatever you do, I will support you and accompany you. You play the qin while I play the se. How happy and harmonious we are!

From the 2nd Stanza of *Roosters Crow at Dawn*,
Odes of Zheng, *Classic of Poetry*

【Commentary】

The poem is about a newly married couple. It has three stanzas. It depicts the newly married couple who loves and lives in harmony with each other. The use of the qin and the se in describing the harmony between the husband and the wife at the end of the poem has exerted profound influence on traditional Chinese culture. The later generations like to draw an analogy between the qin and the se and the harmonious marital relationship. Ancient scholars hoped to achieve academic success by becoming government officials and discharge their official duty to enjoy their family life when getting old. It's their ideal life mode.

37. 狡童

【原文】

彼狡童兮，不与我言兮。维子之故，使我不能餐兮。

《诗经·郑风·狡童》首章

【释文】

滑头的小伙子，不肯再和我说话。因为他的缘故，我吃饭都吃不下。

【解析】

这是一首女子失恋之诗，描写女子在与恋人闹别扭后的娇嗔和不安。诗共两章。女子因恋人不与自己说话、共餐而怄气，焦虑不安，白天茶饭不思吃不下，夜晚辗转反侧睡不安，体现了青年男女恋爱中的细腻情感。

37. The Sly Young Man

The sly young man, he does not want to talk to me any longer. Because of him, I have lost my appetite.

From the 1st Stanza of *The Sly Young Man*,
Odes of Zheng, *Classic of Poetry*

【Commentary】

The poem is about a lovelorn girl. The girl is disturbed after falling out with her love. It has two stanzas. The girl is irritated and loses her appetite in the daytime and cannot fall asleep at night because her love does not talk to her any longer. The poem describes the subtle emotions between young men and young women who are in love.

詩經選譯

褰裳

Roll Your Trousers Up

38. 褰裳

【原文】

子惠思我，褰裳涉溱。子不我思，岂无他人？狂童之狂也且！

《诗经·郑风·褰裳》首章

【释文】

你思恋我的时候，提起衣裳就跨过溱河。你不想我了，难道没有别人追求我吗？你真是太愚昧狂妄了！

【解析】

这是一首女子失恋之诗。诗共两章。郑国诗歌是具有地方色彩的新曲调，被认为激越活泼，抒情细腻，尤其在抒写男女情感方面因表现得非常大胆、直露而被称作“淫诗”。此诗虽写女子的失恋，但女主人公却表现出了一种通达和坚强的意气，与《狡童》中女主人公无法排遣忧思大不相同。

38.Roll Your Trousers Up

You rolled your trousers up and crossed the Zhen River in the old days when you loved me. You do not love me anymore, but don't I have other admirers? How arrogant and stupid you are!

From the 1st Stanza of *Roll Your Trousers Up*,

Odes of Zheng, *Classic of Poetry*

【Commentary】

The poem is about a lovelorn girl. It has two stanzas. The odes of Zheng are of local features and vivid in expressing feelings. In particular, they are explicit in describing the feelings between men and women, so they are called obscene poems. Although the poem is about a lovelorn girl, the girl is sanguine and strong, strikingly different from the girl in *The Sly Young Man*.

39. 风雨

【原文】

风雨如晦，鸡鸣不已。既见君子，云胡不喜？

《诗经·郑风·风雨》三章

【释文】

天地昏暗并且有狂风暴雨，但公鸡仍然准时报晓。我的丈夫已经回家了，我还有什么不欢喜呢？

【解析】

这是一首写妻子与丈夫久别重逢的诗歌。诗共三章。诗歌以风雨交加时，公鸡准时报晓来比兴妻子对丈夫的守候期待。“风雨如晦，鸡鸣不已”这两句诗，在中国传统文化上的意义尤大，“风雨如晦”用以比喻现实的困境，而“鸡鸣不已”则指克服困难、努力进取，这是有气节的士人用作自励的写照。

39.A Tempest

The sky is shrouded with dark clouds and a tempest is coming, but roosters are still crowing at dawn. My husband has come back home. How can I not feel joyful?

From the 3rd Stanza of *A Tempest*,
Odes of Zheng, *Classic of Poetry*

【Commentary】

The poem is about the wife who reunites with her husband after being apart for a long time. It has three stanzas. The poem uses roosters that crow at dawn as affective images to show that the wife is expecting her husband. The lines "the sky is shrouded with dark clouds and a tempest is coming, but roosters are still crowing at dawn" have great significance in the traditional Chinese culture. The first line "the sky is shrouded with dark clouds and a tempest is coming" is used as a metaphor for real-life predicaments while the second line "roosters are still crowing at dawn" refers to overcoming difficulties and forging ahead, which has been widely used by scholars of integrity for self-motivation.

詩經選譯

子衿

Your Collar

40. 子衿

【原文】

青青子衿，悠悠我心。纵我不往，子宁不嗣音？

《诗经·郑风·子衿》首章

【释文】

你的衣领颜色青青，我心里一直都思念你。纵然我没去找你，难道你就不能给我个音信吗？

【解析】

这是一位女子思念情人的诗歌。诗共三章。中国人重视礼仪，言行举止多以礼仪约束，避免过或不及而趋于中庸之美。在男女情感的表达上，也仍然遵循含蓄委婉。但此诗主人公在表达对爱人的思慕之情时，却显得积极主动、热烈奔放。这种张扬大胆的抒情方式，也极大地影响了此后中国文学在这一方面的创作。

40.Your Collar

Your collar is of bluish-green color. I've been missing you all the time. Even if I have not gone to your place, why cannot you send me a message?

From the 1st Stanza of *Your Collar*,
Odes of Zheng, *Classic of Poetry*

【Commentary】

The poem is about the girl who misses her love. It has three stanzas. Chinese people have always attached great importance to rites and their conduct is constrained by them in order to achieve the beauty of the mean. Chinese people are restrained in expressing love. However, the heroine in the poem is proactive and full of passion in expressing her feelings. The explicit ways of expressing emotions have extensive influence on the later Chinese literary creation.

41. 扬之水

【原文】

扬之水，不流束楚。终鲜兄弟，维予与女。无信人之言，人实迋女。

《诗经·郑风·扬之水》首章

【释文】

河水缓缓地流淌，冲不散一捆荆条。我们家里兄弟少，只有我和你同心。你不要轻信别人的谎话，人家是在欺骗你。

【解析】

这是夫妻将要分别时，丈夫对妻子的叮嘱之诗。诗共两章。诗歌以河水漂束楚起兴，水流轻浅就无法冲散成捆的荆条，就好像流言蜚语，不轻信就无事，若是轻信他人挑拨之言，就会给家庭带来破坏。诗中特别提到夫家兄弟少而流言更容易兴起之事，这也可以看出中国人非常重视宗族血缘的关系。此外，中国古语常说“妻贤夫祸少”，说贤惠的妻子总能提醒或者帮助丈夫得体地处理邻里、家庭等事务，以消除许多灾祸，此诗也反映了这方面的情况。

41. The River Flows Slowly

The river flows so slowly that it cannot break up a bundle of wood. I don't have many siblings, and only you and I are with one heart. Do not believe others' lies for they are cheating you.

From the 1st Stanza of *The River Flows Slowly*,
Odes of Zheng, *Classic of Poetry*

【Commentary】

The poem is about the husband who advises his wife before parting. It has two stanzas. The poem uses the river that flows too slowly to break up a bundle of wood as an affective image to show that gossip will do no harm if it's not being paid attention to. Otherwise, harmony of a family will be destroyed. The fact that Chinese people attach great importance to clan relations is reflected in the lines that the husband has few siblings, yet gossip is more likely to be spread. An old Chinese saying goes that the husband who has a virtuous wife will avoid big trouble. A virtuous wife always reminds her husband or helps him to properly handle neighborhood and family affairs, so big trouble is avoided. The poem has also painted such scenarios.

詩經選譯

出其东门

Outside of the Eastern City Gate

42. 出其东门

【原文】

出其东门，有女如云。虽则如云，匪我思存。缟衣綦巾，聊乐我员。

《诗经·郑风·出其东门》首章

【释文】

走出东城门，看到外面的女子多得像天上的浮云。虽然女子很多，但她们都不是我爱慕的人。那位穿白衣青裙的女子，才是我喜爱的人。

【解析】

这是男子表示对妻子忠贞不渝的爱情的诗歌。诗共两章。男子出门在外，可以遇到很多美丽的女子，这些女子多得像天上的浮云，但他心中却不受诱惑，对妻子忠贞。

42.Outside of the Eastern City Gate

After walking outside of the eastern city gate, I find that girls there are as countless as floating clouds. Although there are a big number of them, I admire none but the girl in white shirt and cyan skirt.

From the 1st Stanza of *Outside of the Eastern City Gate*, *Odes of Zheng*, *Classic of Poetry*

【Commentary】

The poem is about the husband who is faithful to his wife. It has two stanzas. Away from home, the husband comes across numerous beautiful girls. They are as countless as floating clouds, but the husband can resist temptations and remain faithful to his wife.

43. 野有蔓草

【原文】

野有蔓草，零露漙兮。有美一人，清扬婉兮。邂逅相遇，适我愿兮。

《诗经·郑风·野有蔓草》首章

【释文】

野地上的青草随意蔓延，叶子上沾有圆圆的露珠。有位独自徘徊的美女，眉清目秀的模样。在路上碰巧遇见她，她真是合我的心意。

【解析】

这是一首男女相恋的诗歌。诗共两章。在人性纯朴的时代，又值仲春时节，男女青年大胆追求自己的意中人。

43.Wild Grass Sprawls

Wild grass sprawls. Its blades are covered with round dew. A beautiful girl is wandering; she has dark eyes and shaped eyebrows. I come across the girl in the street and she's my cup of tea.

From the 1st Stanza of *Wild Grass Sprawls*,

Odes of Zheng, *Classic of Poetry*

【Commentary】

The poem depicts love between young people. It has two stanzas. In the age when human nature was simple and when it was the mid-spring, young men and young women were bold in pursuing their beloved ones.

詩經選譯

溱洧

The Zhen River and the Wei River

44. 溱洧

【原文】

溱与洧，方涣涣兮。士与女，方秉蕑兮。女曰：“观乎？”士曰：“既且。”“且往观乎！洧之外，洵訏且乐。”维士与女，伊其相谑，赠之以勺药。

《诗经·郑风·溱洧》首章

【释文】

溱水和洧水，三月绿波荡漾。春游的男男女女，手里拿着兰草。姑娘说：“咱们去看看吗？”小伙子说：“我已经看过了。”“陪我再去看看吧！洧水的那边，地大又好玩。”男男女女来游玩，他们相互调笑，赠送芍药结良缘。

【解析】

这是一首男女青年恋爱相会的诗歌。诗共两章。农历三月三日是郑国的上巳节，到了这天，人们结伴去水边沐浴以祓除污垢并消除不祥，男女青年也可以借此机会来寻找意中人。诗中“秉蕑”体现了祭祀祈福的思想，而男女青年相赠芍药，则是爱情的象征。

44.The Zhen River and the Wei River

The Zhen River and the Wei River have reflections of green trees in the mid-spring. Men and women hold fragrant thoroughwort for spring outing. One young lady says to her young male companion: "Let's go and have a look." The young man replies: "I've already seen it." The girl says, "Please come with me. The areas over the River Wei are spacious and there are many interesting activities." Young men and young women come to play. They laugh and give each other Chinese herbaceous peonies as a token of love.

From the 1st Stanza of *The Zhen River and the Wei River*,
Odes of Zheng, *Classic of Poetry*

【Commentary】

The poem is about young men and young women who date each other. It has two stanzas. The 3rd day of the 3rd lunar month was the Shangsi Festival in the State of Zheng. On the festival, people went to riverside with their families and friends and bathed in the river to eliminate dirt and ill omens. Young men and young women took the advantage of the festival to find their love. Holding fragrant thoroughwort was a ritual of offering sacrifices to Heaven and ancestors and praying for blessings while giving Chinese herbaceous peonies to each other was a token of love.

45. 南山

【原文】

析薪如之何？匪斧不克。取妻如之何？匪媒不得。既曰得止，曷又极止？

《诗经·齐风·南山》四章

【释文】

用什么工具来劈柴？没有斧头办不到。怎么才能娶到妻子？一定需要媒人来帮忙。既然你已经娶了她，为何还让她回娘家？

【解析】

这是一首讽刺齐襄公与同父异母妹妹文姜淫乱的诗。诗共四章。诗歌以劈柴须用斧头起兴，认为娶妻也需要有媒人才能办好。中国是一个重视礼仪的国度，在婚姻上尤其如此，须要按照各种礼仪聘娶妻子，才能得到家庭、社会的承认。兄妹淫乱，不合礼制，为社会所不齿。

45.The South Mountain

How can you chop firewood? You cannot do so without an axe. How can you marry a wife? You need the help of matchmakers. Since you have married her, why allow her to go back to her parents' home?

From the 4th Stanza of *The South Mountain*,

Odes of Qi, *Classic of Poetry*

【Commentary】

The poem is about Duke Xiang of Qi who committed incest with his half-sister Wenjiang. It has four stanzas. The poem uses axes that are necessary tools for chopping firewood as affective images to show that matchmakers are the key to marrying a wife. Rituals have enjoyed paramount importance in China, so a host of rituals should be observed in order to marry a woman. Marriages cannot gain recognition of the family and the whole society unless they go through certain rituals. Incest does not conform to rituals and is despised by the whole society.

詩經選譯

载驱

The Carriage Is Driven at Full Speed

46. 载驱

【原文】

载驱薄薄，簟茀朱鞹。鲁道有荡，齐子发夕。

《诗经·齐风·载驱》首章

【释文】

车马奔驰轰隆隆，那个车子有竹制的车帘和红漆兽皮的车盖。鲁国的道路平坦宽广，齐女却从早拖到晚都不肯嫁过来。

【解析】

这是一首齐女文姜出嫁的诗。诗共四章。文姜嫁给鲁庄公，但迟迟不肯入境，目的是要庄公远离媵妾。在周代，诸侯娶一国之女为夫人，女方须以侄（兄弟之女）娣（妹妹）随嫁，同时还须从另两个与女方同姓之国各请一位女子陪嫁，亦各以侄、娣相从，一共九人，只有夫人处于正妻地位，其余都属于妾。但齐国是大国，鲁国是小国，所以文姜才会提出这种要求。

46.The Carriage Is Driven at Full Speed

The carriage is driven at full speed, making a loud noise. The carriage has a bamboo curtain and hide-covered roof with red lacquer. Roads in the State of Lu are wide and flat, but the girl from the State of Qi is unwilling to marry into the family of Lu, so she has postponed her wedding again and again.

From the 1st Stanza of *The Carriage Is Driven at Full Speed*, *Odes of Qi*, *Classic of Poetry*

【Commentary】

The poem is about Wenjiang, the girl of Qi who is going to get married. It has four stanzas. Wenjiang was supposed to marry Duke Zhuang of Lu, but she was reluctant to enter the State of Lu for she wanted to force Duke Zhuang to distance himself from the accompanying concubines. During the period of the Zhou Dynasty, when a duke married his wife, a total of eight girls, including the daughters of the bride's brothers and the bride's younger sisters, and another two girls from the bride's state would marry the duke together with the bride as concubines. As the State of Qi was a big country while the State of Lu was a small one, Wenjiang could make this request.

47. 硕鼠

【原文】

硕鼠硕鼠，无食我黍！三岁贯女，莫我肯顾。逝将去女，适彼乐土。乐土乐土，爰得我所！

《诗经·魏风·硕鼠》首章

【释文】

大老鼠啊大老鼠，不要吃我的黄黍！我多年劳动养活你，你却不顾我的死活。我发誓要离开你，前往快乐的地方。乐土啊新乐土，那里才是我的好去处！

【解析】

这是一首控诉统治者贪婪无厌的诗歌。诗共三章。这首诗把不劳而获的统治者比喻成无情无义的大老鼠。这位诗人有怨恨，更有实际的反抗行为，他决定以逃亡的方式来控诉这个不公平的社会。

47.Large Rats

Large rats! Large rats! Do not eat my millet any more. I have fed you for all these years through my toils, but you have felt no pity for me even if I have great difficulty in making ends meet. I swear that I will leave you for a happy place. A happy place! A happy place! That is where I should go.

From the 1st Stanza of *Large Rats*,
Odes of Wei, *Classic of Poetry*

【Commentary】

The poem denounces the insatiably greedy rulers. It has three stanzas. Analogy between ruthless large rats and rulers who reap without sowing is drawn to show that the poet is resentful and attempts to denounce the unfair society by fleeing.

詩經選譯

绸缪

Intertwined Firewood

48. 绸缪

【原文】

绸缪束薪，三星在天。今夕何夕，见此良人？子兮子兮，如此良人何？

《诗经·唐风·绸缪》首章

【释文】

柴草紧紧缠缚，天上星光闪耀。今天是什么好日子，嫁了称心如意的夫婿了？你呀你呀，要怎么与丈夫共度良宵呢？

【解析】

这是一首祝贺新婚的诗。诗共三章。诗以薪起兴，形成中国古代以薪言男女婚姻的传统。因为古代娶妻多在黄昏，以燃薪照明，人们逐渐以“束薪”等词代指婚姻礼俗。

48.Intertwined Firewood

Firewood is tightly bound. Stars are twinkling in the sky. How auspicious today is! You have married your ideal husband. Girl, girl, how will you spend the wedding night with your husband?

From the 1st Stanza of *Intertwined Firewood,*

Odes of Tang, Classic of Poetry

【Commentary】

The poem is about congratulations on newlyweds. It has three stanzas. The use of firewood as an affective image started the tradition of using firewood as a metaphor for marriage in ancient China. As most of the ancient Chinese get married at dusk, they burned firewood for illumination. "Bound firewood" has been gradually used to refer to wedding ceremonies.

詩經選譯

鸨羽
Wings of Bustards

49. 鸨羽

【原文】

肃肃鸨羽，集于苞栩。王事靡盬，不能艺稷黍。父母何怙？悠悠苍天，曷其有所？

《诗经·唐风·鸨羽》首章

【释文】

鸨鸟展开翅膀发出沙沙的响声，栖息在栎树丛上。周王的徭役没完没了，使我不能回家种黍粱。父母依靠谁生活？高高在上的苍天啊，我什么时候才能回家？

【解析】

这是一首控诉徭役的诗。诗共三章。中国古代的农民经常被征调来服徭役，没完没了的徭役，使他们终年奔波在外，无法安居乐业，赡养父母。中国人重视孝道，有浓厚的家庭观念，父母健在，则不会远行。但因为王事而不能尽孝父母，所以诗人发出呼天怨地的声音，强烈抗议统治者的深重压迫。

49.Wings of Bustards

With a rustle of wings, bustards land on oak trees. Corvee duties of the king of Zhou are so endless that I cannot return home to grow millet and sorghum. Who can my old parents depend on? Oh, Heaven, when can I go home?

From the 1st Stanza of *Wings of Bustards,*
Odes of Tang, Classic of Poetry

【Commentary】

The poem denounces corvee duties. It has three stanzas. In ancient China, peasants were often conscripted for corvee duties. The endless corvee duties forced them to stay far away from home and deprived their rights of enjoying their family life and taking care of their parents. Chinese people have attached great importance to filial duty, so they would not go on a long journey when their parents were alive. However, they could not fulfill their filial duty because of corvee duties for the sovereign. Therefore, the poet strongly protested against oppression.

50. 葛生

【原文】

夏之日，冬之夜。百岁之后，归于其居！

《诗经·唐风·葛生》四章

【释文】

夏季白日太长，而冬天则长夜漫漫。只有在我死后，才能与你在坟墓里再相逢！

【解析】

这是一首悼亡诗歌。诗共五章。诗歌先写到白天与黑夜给人带来的矛盾，嫌白天太长，无法消除对亲人离世的思念，所以渴望黑夜，希望在睡眠中暂时忘记痛苦；但到了晚上，却又睡不着，辗转反侧，所以又希望白天早点到来。唯一的期待只能是死后，两个人能够在一起，永远不分开。生时不能相聚，死后期待相逢，这也是古代中国人的习惯思维。

50.Lush Kudzu Vines

The day is long in the summer while the night is lengthy in the winter. I cannot reunite with you in the tomb until the day I die.

From the 4th Stanza of *Lush Kudzu Vines,*

Odes of Tang, Classic of Poetry

【Commentary】

The poem is about mourning the deceased spouse. It has five stanzas. The poet describes his ambivalent attitude towards the day and the night. The poet terribly misses his deceased spouse in the day, so he longs for the night wishing that sleep could temporarily ease the pain. But he can not fall asleep at night, so he wishes the day could come early. His only hope is to be buried with his love after death, so they will not be separated any longer. Ancient Chinese hope that if they cannot stay together when alive, they can reunite after death.

51. 小戎

【原文】

小戎俴收，五楘梁辀。游环胁驱，阴靷鋈续。文茵畅毂，驾我骐馵。言念君子，温其如玉。在其板屋，乱我心曲。

《诗经 · 秦风 · 小戎》首章

【释文】

战车轻小车厢浅，用五根皮条缠绕车辕。用皮环皮扣来固定车马，用白铜环来装饰拉车的皮带。用虎皮做成的坐垫和长长的车轴，驾驶着花纹相杂的马车。想起我出征在外的丈夫，他的人品温和如美玉。如今他从军到了西戎，这让我心烦意乱。

【解析】

这是一位妇女思念她远征的丈夫的诗歌。诗共三章。诗歌回想起丈夫驾战车出征的情形，虽是战车，但装饰得整齐亮丽，可见她的丈夫是一位严谨的士兵。诗以玉写人，影响深远，此后，中国人认为玉具有仁、义、智、勇、洁五种品德，应当都是受《诗经》的启示。

51.Small Chariots

The chariot is small and light and the compartment is not spacious. Five leather straps twine the shafts; leather rings and leather buckles are used to fix the chariot and horses. White copper rings are used to decorate the leather straps that pull the chariot. The cushion is made of tiger skin and the axle is long. It reminds me of my husband who is on a military expedition. He is as mild as jade. He is on a military expedition to Xirong, which upsets me.

From the 1st Stanza of *Small Chariots,*
Odes of Qin, Classic of Poetry

【Commentary】

The poem is about the wife who misses her husband who is on a military expedition. It has three stanzas. In the poem, the wife recalls the scenario when her husband goes on an expedition on a chariot. Although it is a chariot, it is beautifully decorated, indicating that her husband is conscientious. The analogy between a person's character and jade has profound influence. The five virtues of jade, namely, humanity, righteousness, wisdom, valor and pure believed by Chinese are originally from the *Classic of Poetry*.

詩經選譯

蒹葭

Reeds

52. 蒹葭

【原文】

蒹葭苍苍，白露为霜。所谓伊人，在水一方。溯洄从之，道阻且长。溯游从之，宛在水中央。

《诗经·秦风·蒹葭》首章

【释文】

河边的芦苇长得茂盛青苍，秋天的白露已经结成了霜。我所爱慕的意中人，就在河水的那一边。我逆着河流去寻找她，但道路却险阻悠长。我顺着河流寻找她，她好像又在河水的中央。

【解析】

这是一首追求意中人不得的诗歌。诗共三章。诗中写诗人追求的“伊人”行止飘忽不定，难以接近。诗歌的意义在于启示我们，在追求理想的过程中，总会遇到各种曲折艰难，只有克服困难，才能收获美好的东西。

52.Reeds

Reeds along the river are luxuriant. White dew in the autumn has become frost. My love, she is on the other side of the river. I want to search for her upstream, but the road is long and dangerous. I want to search for her downstream, but she seems to be in the center of the river.

From the 1st Stanza of *Reeds,*
Odes of Qin, Classic of Poetry

【Commentary】

The poem is about the young man who fails to win the heart of the girl he loves. It has three stanzas. The girl described in the poem is elusive and hard to approach. From the poem, we realize that there are a variety of difficulties in the process of pursuing our goals and we cannot reap the rewards unless we overcome all the difficulties.

詩經選譯

黄鸟

Siskins

53. 黄鸟

【原文】

交交黄鸟，止于棘。谁从穆公？子车奄息。维此奄息，百夫之特。临其穴，惴惴其栗。彼苍者天，歼我良人！如可赎兮，人百其身！

《诗经·秦风·黄鸟》首章

【释文】

黄雀发出交交的哀鸣声，飞落在酸枣树枝上。是谁追随秦穆公殉葬了？就是那个子车奄息。子车奄息啊，他的才德没有人能比得上。走近奄息的墓穴，让人战栗心惊。苍天不公平啊，灭亡我们的好善人！如果可以赎回他，我们愿死一百次来抵命！

【解析】

这是秦国人挽“三良”的诗歌。诗共三章。秦穆公死后，以秦国的三位良臣子车氏之三子奄息、仲行、铖虎陪葬，秦人对此深感痛心。诗歌不仅表达了对贤人的同情，而且也对这种野蛮的殉葬习俗进行控诉。

53.Siskins

Siskins give mournful cries. They alight on the branches of jujube trees. Who have been buried alive with the deceased Duke Mu of Qin? It was Ziche Yanxi. Oh, Ziche Yanxi, his talents and virtue dwarfed all the others. All those who approach the tomb of Ziche Yanxi are terror-stricken. Heaven, how unfair you are! You have killed the good man! If we could die in his stead, we would be willing to die a hundred times for his survival.

From the 1st Stanza of *Siskins,*
Odes of Qin, Classic of Poetry

【Commentary】

The elegy was made by Qin people for three virtuous men. It has three stanzas. After the death of Duke Mu of Qin, three sons of Ziche, the three virtuous officials, Yanxi, Zhongxing, and Zhenhu were buried alive with the dead duke. Qin people were grieved at their death. The poem has not only expressed sympathy for the virtuous men, but also denounced the barbarian practice of human sacrifice.

54．晨风

【原文】

山有苞棣，隰有树檖。未见君子，忧心如醉。如何如何？忘我实多！

《诗经·秦风·晨风》三章

【释文】

山上长满了棣树，洼地长有山梨树。没有看见我的丈夫，我心里忧愁得就像喝醉了酒。我应该怎么办呀？或许他早已经把我忘记了！

【解析】

这是一位妇女疑心被丈夫抛弃的诗歌。诗共三章。诗先以山上树木丛生起兴，大自然生机勃勃，但这位妇女心中却如醉酒一般无精打采，原因是她的丈夫外出太久，又毫无音讯，从而感觉自己被丈夫抛弃了。

54.Sparrow Hawks

The mountains are covered with kerria japonica trees while the low-lying land is overlaid with mountain ashes. As I cannot see my husband, I am dispirited as if I were drunk. What should I do? Maybe my husband has already forgotten me.

From the 3rd Stanza of *Sparrow Hawk,*
Odes of Qin, Classic of Poetry

【Commentary】

The poem is about the wife who suspects that she has been abandoned by her husband. It has three stanzas. The poem starts with trees in the mountains as affective images. The nature is full of vitality while the lady is dispirited as if she were drunk because she's afraid that she is abandoned by her husband who has been away for a long time with no news.

詩經選譯

无衣

No Armor

55. 无衣

【原文】

岂曰无衣？与子同袍。王于兴师，修我戈矛，与子同仇！

《诗经·秦风·无衣》首章

【释文】

怎么能说没有衣服穿呢？我和你合穿一件战袍。君王要起兵打仗，我们修理好戈矛，共同对付入侵的敌人！

【解析】

这是一首秦地的军中战歌。诗共三章。全诗充满慷慨激昂、热情互助的气氛，表现战士们英勇抗敌的精神。大约在公元前771年，因周幽王无道而导致外族入侵镐京，秦人靠近京畿，与周王室休戚相关，遂奋起反抗。周王虽昏庸，但士兵踊跃杀敌，抵抗外族，表现了强烈的爱国主义精神。“同袍”一词也成了战友的代名词。

55.No Armor

How can you say you have no armor to wear? I will share mine with you. The sovereign wants to raise an army for war, so let's fix our dagger-axes and spears to fight against the invaders.

From the 1st Stanza of *No Armor,*

Odes of Qin, Classic of Poetry

【Commentary】

The poem is a battle song in the territory of Qin. It has three stanzas. The poem depicts soldiers who are full of fighting spirit and ready to help each other. Zhou Dynasty was invaded in 771 B.C. due to the tyrannical ruling of King You of Zhou. Qin people approached the capital of Zhou, intending to invade Zhou Dynasty. The Zhou Dynasty was on the brink of collapse. Though the king was fatuous, his soldiers were brave and patriotic. "Shared armor" has become a byword for battle companions.

56. 渭阳

【原文】

我送舅氏，曰至渭阳。何以赠之？路车乘黄。

《诗经·秦风·渭阳》首章

【释文】

我依依不舍地送别舅舅，一直送到渭水的北边。拿什么礼物送给舅舅呢？只有一辆大车和四匹黄马。

【解析】

这是一首外甥送舅父的送别诗。诗共两章。诗中写外甥送舅父送到渭水边，而所送的礼物有车有马，可见甥舅之间的感情非常深厚。之所以用车马作为礼物送人，是因为国家的强弱往往以战车、战马的多少来衡量。不过，先秦时期，诸侯国之间多以婚姻结成政治联盟，彼此借重，所以，甥舅之间的感情也不仅仅是人伦之间的感情，有时也是一种政治的谋略。

56.North of the Wei River

I feel reluctant to say goodbye to my uncle, so I accompany him to the north of the Wei River. What presents have I prepared for my uncle? I have nothing but a big carriage and four yellow horses for him.

From the 1st Stanza of *North of the Wei River,*
Odes of Qin, Classic of Poetry

【Commentary】

The poem is about the nephew who sees off his uncle. It has two stanzas. The nephew accompanies his uncle to the north of the Wei River and gives him a carriage and four horses as presents, which show the nephew has a deep affection for his uncle. Carriages and horses are given as presents because the strength of a country is judged by the number of chariots and war horses. In the pre-Qin period, marriage was used for political alliance between vassal states, so the nephew's affection for his uncle is not only personal, but also a political strategy in such a context.

57. 衡门

【原文】

岂其食鱼，必河之鲂？岂其取妻，必齐之姜？

《诗经·陈风·衡门》二章

【释文】

难道我们吃鱼，一定要吃河中的鲂鱼吗？难道我们娶妻子，一定要娶齐国的姜姓女子吗？

【解析】

这是一位没落贵族安于贫贱、自我宽慰的诗。诗共三章。这位贵族有过风光体面的日子，可以吃最好的东西，也可以娶最美的女子为妻。然而落魄以后就只能自我安慰了。春秋时，齐国的统治者姓姜，齐国是当时的强国，也是当时众多诸侯国联姻的首选之国，所以诗以齐姜代指美女。当然，如果抛开这个背景来看这个诗的话，诗歌倒是给我们一些启示：人世间的佳肴、美女并非都适合于每个人，我们只需要找到适合于自己的，那就是最好的。

57.The Doorframe Made of Slats

We eat fish, but must we eat gurnards in the river? We marry wives, but must we marry girls with the family name "Jiang" from the State of Qi?

From the 2nd Stanza of *The Doorframe Made of Slats, Odes of Chen, Classic of Poetry*

【Commentary】

The poem is about the impoverished aristocrat who comforts himself with the thought that one should feel content to remain poor. It has three stanzas. The aristocrat used to live a prosperous life when he could eat the most delicious food and marry the most beautiful girl, but he has to comfort himself after impoverishment. During the Spring and Autumn period, the family name of the rulers of Qi was Jiang. As the State of Qi was powerful, it was the first choice for other vassal sates to forge alliance through marriage, so "Qi Jiang" referred to beauties in the poem. If we read the poem outside of the context, we can learn from the poem that not all the delicacies and beauties are fit for everyone. The best are those that suit us.

詩經選譯

月出

The Moon Has Come out

58. 月出

【原文】

月出皎兮，佼人僚兮，舒窈纠兮，劳心悄兮！

《诗经·陈风·月出》首章

【释文】

月亮出来月光皎洁，月下的美人更娇美，她苗条又娴雅，让我思念心烦忧！

【解析】

这是一首月夜怀人的诗。诗共三章。诗写夜月初升而思及爱人，其迷离朦胧的意境和忧伤的感情，对中国文化影响尤大。此后的文人或因游学仕宦，或因其他种种原因，往往不能与家人团聚，常借明月的团圆来反衬诗人之孤独。

58.The Moon Has Come out

The moon has come out and the moonlight is bright. The beautiful girl is more attractive under the moonlight. She is slim and graceful. How terribly I miss her!

From the 1st Stanza of *The Moon Has Come out,*
Odes of Chen, Classic of Poetry

【Commentary】

The poem is about missing a girl on a moonlit night. It has three stanzas. The moonlit night put the poet in mind of his love. The indistinct scene and melancholy mood have profound influence on Chinese culture. Scholars of later generations often use the round moon as sharp contrast to their loneliness if they can not reunite with their families due to studying or working as officials in other places or other reasons.

59. 株林

【原文】

胡为乎株林？从夏南！匪适株林，从夏南！

《诗经·陈风·株林》首章

【释文】

为什么要到株林去？以为是跟着夏南去游玩！实际上他到株林来，不是真的找夏南！

【解析】

这是一首讽刺陈灵公与夏姬淫乱的诗。诗共两章。诗中“夏南”是陈大夫御叔之子夏征舒，他的母亲夏姬则是一个淫荡的美妇，与陈灵公及大臣孔宁、仪行父均私通。诗中所描绘的，就是陈灵公及其大臣到株林与夏姬相会的事情。人们对这种伤风败俗的行径深恶痛绝，所以作诗以讽。

59.Outskirts of Zhu

Why does he go to the outskirts of Zhu? I guess he goes there for Xia Nan. But it's not for Xia Nan that he goes to the outskirts of Zhu.

From the 1st Stanza of *Outskirts of Zhu,*
Odes of Chen, Classic of Poetry

【Commentary】

The poem satirizes fornication committed by Duke Ling of Chen and Xia Ji. It has two stanzas. Xia Nan in the poem referred to Xia Zhengshu, son of Yushu, a high-ranking official of Chen. Xia Nan's mother Xia Ji was a beautiful yet licentious woman, who committed fornication with Duke Ling of Chen and his two high-ranking officials Kong Ning and Yi Xingfu. The poem depicts a secret rendezvous between Duke Ling of Chen and his officials and Xia Ji at the outskirts of Zhu. People have always abhorred such immoral behavior, so the poem satirizes such behavior.

詩經選譯

隰有苌楚

Kiwifruit Trees in the Low-lying Wetland

60. 隰有苌楚

【原文】

隰有苌楚，猗傩其枝。夭之沃沃，乐子之无知！

《诗经·桧风·隰有苌楚》首章

【释文】

低湿地里长满了羊桃，树枝婀娜多姿。树木长得细嫩有光泽，我爱慕你的纯真和淳朴啊！

【解析】

这是女子爱慕一个未婚的男子的恋歌。诗共三章。诗歌以低湿地上长出鲜嫩的羊桃起兴，写一位女子对纯真淳朴的男子的爱慕之情。在中国文化里，对真诚坦率、保有赤子之心的人非常欣赏；而对那些在世俗社会中变得机心重重的人，多不持赞赏的态度。诗中这位男子，正如山间的草木一样纯真淳朴，这正是这个女子所爱慕的。

60.Kiwifruit Trees in the Low-lying Wetland

The low-lying wetland is covered with kiwifruit trees. Their branches are beautiful and leaves are green and shiny. I admire you for your innocence and genuineness.

From the 1st Stanza of *Kiwifruit Trees in the Low-lying Wetland, Odes of Kuai, Classic of Poetry*

【Commentary】

The poem is about the girl who falls in love with a young single man. It has three stanzas. The poem uses green kiwifruit trees as affective images at the beginning to depict the admiration of the girl for an unsophisticated and genuine young man. Chinese culture approves those who are sincere and straightforward while disproves those who are scheming. The young man in the poem is as artless as trees and grass in the mountain and such qualities are the reasons why the girl admires him.

61. 鸤鸠

【原文】

鸤鸠在桑，其子七兮。淑人君子，其仪一兮。其仪一兮，心如结兮。

《诗经·曹风·鸤鸠》首章

【释文】

布谷鸟在桑树上筑巢，无私地喂养七只小鸟儿。那些善良有才德的好君子，他们的言行都是一致的。他们表里如一，忠诚之心如磐石般坚固。

【解析】

这是赞美在位统治者的诗。诗共四章。诗歌以鸤鸠有七子起兴，飞鸟有七子，但人的言行必须表里如一。中国人讲究忠信诚实，待人诚恳，言必信，行必果，这是淑人君子应当具备的最基本美德。

61.Cuckoos

Cuckoos build their nests on mulberry trees in order to selflessly feed their seven baby birds. The kind and virtuous men match their words to their deeds and their faithful hearts are as firm as rocks.

From the 1st Stanza of *Cuckoos,*
Odes of Cao, Classic of Poetry

【Commentary】

The poem eulogizes the incumbent ruler. It has four stanzas. The poem uses cuckoos that have seven children as affective images to show that a person should suit his action to his words. Chinese stress faith and honesty. Being genuine to others and being true in word and resolute in deed are the basic qualities of a noble man.

62. 下泉

【原文】

洌彼下泉，浸彼苞稂。忾我寤叹，念彼周京。

《诗经·曹风·下泉》首章

【释文】

地下的泉水非常冷冽，淹泡得粱草都难以生长。我睡醒之后心中充满了感慨，总是想念以往稳定的京城。

【解析】

这是曹人赞美晋国的诗。诗共四章。春秋末期，周王室内乱，晋文公派人护持周王室，得到曹人的赞美。东周初期，周天子对天下诸侯尚有相当的约束力，天下也相对太平。但自从天子失政之后，诸侯争霸，天下动荡，百姓失所，人民思念周京，也就是对太平社会的期待。

62.Spring Water

Spring water from the underground source is very cold. Grass soaked in the spring water is hard to grow. I feel sad after waking. I constantly miss the peaceful capital in the old days.

From the 1st Stanza of *Spring Water,*

Odes of Cao, Classic of Poetry

【Commentary】

The poem is about Cao people who extolled the State of Jin. It has four stanzas. At the end of the Spring and Autumn period, commotion broke out in the Zhou Dynasty, so Duke Wen of Jin sent his troops to protect the royal family of Zhou, which gained laudation of Cao people. In the beginning of the Eastern Zhou, kings could constrain rulers of vassal states, so their people lived in peace. Nevertheless, after the king of Eastern Zhou lost power, rulers of vassal states competed for supremacy, leading common people to be displaced. Common people missed the capital of Eastern Zhou as they aspired to have a peaceful society.

詩經選譯

七月

Seventh Lunar Month

63. 七月

【原文】

二之日凿冰冲冲，三之日纳于凌阴。四之日其蚤，献羔祭韭。九月肃霜，十月涤场。朋酒斯飨，曰杀羔羊。跻彼公堂，称彼兕觥，万寿无疆！

《诗经·豳风·七月》八章

【释文】

腊月里开凿冰块咚咚地响，正月又要送去冰窖里。二月取出冰块来为祭礼作准备，献上韭菜和羊羔作为祭品。九月天高气爽，十月清扫打谷场。用两壶美酒来招待客人，再宰杀羔羊。走进乡亲们集会的公堂上，举起手中的酒杯，齐声高祝万寿无疆！

【解析】

这是叙写西周农民一年辛苦劳作的诗。诗共八章。诗歌写人民终年劳作的情况，这一节则是写他们为贵族统治者大办酒宴、庆贺祝寿的事。中国人有浓厚的尊祖祈福的观念，在年终岁末，往往要祭祀祖先，感谢祖先的保佑与恩赐。

63.Seventh Lunar Month

Ice is cut, making a loud noise in the twelfth lunar month. Ice blocks are sent to icehouses in the first lunar month. Ice blocks are taken out in preparation for sacrificial ceremonies and chives and lambs are offered as sacrifices in the second lunar month. The sky is high and the weather is fine in the ninth lunar month. Threshing ground is cleaned up in the tenth lunar month. Guests are entertained with two bottles of good wine and lamb. I walk into the hall where my town folks are gathering, raising our wine glasses, we cry in unison, wishing our host a long life.

From the 8th Stanza of *July,*

Odes of Bin, Classic of Poetry

【Commentary】

The poem depicts the toil of peasants of Western Zhou throughout the year. It has eight stanzas. The quoted stanza is about holding birthday banquets for the aristocratic rulers. As Chinese people have the time-honored tradition of respecting their ancestors and praying for happiness, they worship their ancestors and show their gratitude to them for their blessings at the end of each year.

詩經選譯

鹿鸣

Deer Bell

64. 鹿鸣

【原文】

呦呦鹿鸣，食野之苹。我有嘉宾，鼓瑟吹笙。吹笙鼓簧，承筐是将。人之好我，示我周行。

《诗经·小雅·鹿鸣》首章

【释文】

鹿儿呦呦地叫唤，在野地上吃着野苹。我有很多的好宾客，大家在宴席上弹瑟吹笙。吹笙按簧奏出欢庆的音乐，捧上礼物送给宾客。出席宴会的宾客都喜爱我，也教给我许多大道理。

【解析】

这是贵族宴请宾客的诗。诗共三章。诗歌以鹿儿呼朋引伴共吃野苹起兴，赞美宴会上的亲朋好友和睦相携，其乐融融。中国重视礼乐文明，礼以节人，乐以感人，古代贵族的宴会上往往演奏音乐以表达彼此的感情志向，用以增进了解，沟通感情，期待睦邻友好、尊卑有序。

64.Deer Bell

Deer bell to invite their friends to eat wormwood on the wild land. I have lots of good guests, who play the se and blow the sheng at dinner parties. Festive music is played and gifts are given to the guests. All of my guests are fond of me and they teach me a lot of philosophies.

From the 1st Stanza of *Deer Bell,*

Lesser Court Hymns, Classic of Poetry

[Commentary]

The poem is about aristocrats who entertain their guests. It has three stanzas. The poem uses deer that bell to invite their friends to eat wormwood on the wild land as affective images to praise the harmony and happiness between friends and relatives at banquet parties. Ancient Chinese people thought highly of rites and music for they believed that rites regularized behavior while music touched the hearts of people. Music was performed to express feelings and aspirations, enhance mutual understanding, deepen their friendship, and maintain hierarchy and order at the ancient aristocratic banquets.

65. 常棣

【原文】

兄弟阋于墙，外御其务。每有良朋，烝也无戎。

《诗经·小雅·常棣》四章

【释文】

兄弟虽在家里争吵，却能一致抵御外侮。平时虽然有好朋友，但危急时刻却难以依靠。

【解析】

这是一首宴请兄弟的诗。诗共八章。兄弟之间虽免不了有摩擦，但是在遇到外侮时，却能保持清醒，顾全大局，一致对外。诗歌第七章写家宴时兄弟齐集，妻子好合，兄弟和睦，反映了中国文化史上“兄弟如手足”的悠长文化传统。

65.Callery Pear Trees

Though brothers fight at home, they unite in the face of external bullies. Though we have good friends in normal times, they cannot be relied on in desperate situations.

From the 4th Stanza of *Callery Pear Trees,*
Lesser Court Hymns, Classic of Poetry

【Commentary】

The poem is about entertaining brothers. It has eight stanzas. Though there're frictions among brothers, they can keep sober-minded and unite to fight against external bullies for the sake of the overall interest. The seventh stanza of the poem is about the family banquet attended by all the brothers. It reflects the traditional idea that "brothers are like one's own hands and feet".

詩經選譯

伐木
Fell Trees

66. 伐木

【原文】

伐木丁丁，鸟鸣嘤嘤。出自幽谷，迁于乔木。嘤其鸣矣，求其友声。相彼鸟矣，犹求友声。矧伊人矣，不求友生？神之听之，终和且平。

《诗经·小雅·伐木》首章

【释文】

砍伐树木时发出丁丁的响声，小鸟嘤嘤地鸣叫。小鸟虽然来自深谷，却飞到高树上筑巢。小鸟嘤嘤地叫唤，是在呼唤朋友。看看这些小鸟儿，它们尚且寻找朋友。何况我们这些人，怎能不结交朋友？天上的神明都能听见我们交友的心声，它定会赐予我们和乐安宁。

【解析】

这是一首宴享亲友故旧的诗歌。诗共三章。诗歌以飞鸟从山谷高飞到高树上建巢起兴，写人应当结交朋友，相互切磋。中国古人很重视交友，而且应当结交比自己优秀的朋友，以提高修养。诗歌中的“出于幽谷，迁于乔木”，就是讲人起步虽低，但可以通过努力来提高学问、道德。

66.Fell Trees

Trees make a loud noise when they are felled. Birds chirp. Though from the deep valley, birds build their nests on the top of tall trees. Birds chirp. They talk to their friends. Look at the birds. They want their friends. We, as human beings, how can we not make friends? Heavenly Deity can read our thought of wanting friends, so he will give us peace and happiness.

From the 1st Stanza of *Fell Trees,*
Lesser Court Hymns, Classic of Poetry

【Commentary】

The poem is about entertaining relatives and friends. It has three stanzas. The poem uses birds that fly from deep valleys to build their nests on the top of high trees as affective images to show that human beings should make friends and learn from each other. Ancient Chinese attached great importance to making friends, especially those who were superior to oneself so as to enhance one's self cultivation. The line "though from the deep valley, birds build their nests on the top of tall trees" means that though starting from a low position, one can improve his learning and standard of morality through his own efforts.

67. 天保

【原文】

如月之恒，如日之升。如南山之寿，不骞不崩。如松柏之茂，无不尔或承。

《诗经·小雅·天保》六章

【释文】

您好像上半夜升起的月亮一样渐满，您如同东升的太阳一样有朝气。您如南山一般高寿，永远不会亏损和崩塌。您如松柏一样茂盛青翠，子子孙孙永远繁衍传承。

【解析】

这是一首臣子祝颂君主的诗。诗共六章。诗歌用了四个比喻来表达美好的祝愿，月恒日升、山高松茂，这都是大自然里恒久不变的现象，用以祝愿短暂的人生。这个祝寿之词，在中国后来的文化里，演变成了“寿比南山不老松”这么简单的一句话，寄寓了人们对长寿的美好期待。

67.Blessings of Heaven

Like the waxing moon in the first half of the night, you are full of strength. Like the rising sun, you are full of vigor. Like the South Mountain that will never fall, you will live an eternal life. Like ever-green pines and cypresses, you will have generation after generation of descendants.

From the 6th Stanza of *Blessings of Heaven,*
Lesser Court Hymns, Classic of Poetry

【Commentary】

The poem is about good wishes expressed by officials to their sovereign. It has six stanzas. Four similes are used to express good wishes. Waxing moon, rising sun, high mountains and ever-green pines and cypresses are natural phenomena. They are used as good wishes to man and have been evolved into one simple sentence "Live a life as long as the evergreen pine on the South Mountain", epitomizing the aspiration for long life.

詩經選譯

采薇
Pick Wild Peas

68. 采薇

【原文】

昔我往矣，杨柳依依。今我来思，雨雪霏霏。行道迟迟，载渴载饥。我心伤悲，莫知我哀！

《诗经·小雅·采薇》六章

【释文】

当初我出征的时候，杨柳枝条随风轻摆。如今我征战归来，大雪却纷纷漫漫。回家的道路泥泞曲折，我也饥渴疲惫。我心里充满了伤悲，但这些悲哀有谁能理解！

【解析】

这是一位守边兵士在归途中写的诗。诗共六章。西周末年，北方少数民族势力强悍，频繁入侵中原。戍守边塞的将士满腔热情，抗击外患，保家卫国。诗歌用对比的手法，先回忆起出征之时天朗气清，归来时则雨雪纷飞，这也暗示了出征时为国征战的踊跃积极，而多年的征战之后则是满腔悲伤。杨柳依依的明丽景色，与悲伤的感情反衬，正是中国文学以乐景写哀情的传统。

68.Pick Wild Peas

Willows wavered in breeze when I went on an expedition while snow is heavy when I come back from the battlefield. The road to my home is muddy and winding and I'm starving, thirsty and exhausted. I'm filled with distress, but who can understand why I'm so grieved?

From the 6th Stanza of *Pick Wild Peas,*
Lesser Court Hymns, Classic of Poetry

【Commentary】

The poem is written by a garrison soldier on his way back home. It has six stanzas. In the late Western Zhou Dynasty, minorities from the north were aggressive and frequently invaded the Central Plains. Troops stationed at the border area were patriotic and fought bravely against foreign invaders to defend their country. The poet first recalled the fine weather when he went on an expedition, which was a sharp contrast to the heavy snow when he came back. By depicting the weather, the poet implied that he was active in going on an expedition against enemies, but distressed after several years' fighting. The sunny days when willows waver in breeze are in stark contrast to sad feelings. It is the tradition of Chinese literature that happy scenes are used to reflect sad emotions.

69. 杕杜

【原文】

陟彼北山，言采其杞。王事靡盬，忧我父母。檀车幝幝，四牡痯痯，征夫不远！

《诗经·小雅·杕杜》三章

【释文】

我登上那座北山，采摘着山上的枸杞。永无休止地为君王服兵役，我心里却担忧家中的父母。用檀木做的兵车已破烂，战马也早已疲惫不堪，征夫回家的日子应该不远了吧！

【解析】

这是一首写征夫思妇的诗。诗共四章。此章写男子为国出征而不能侍奉父母，心中感到忧愁不已。中国人讲忠孝，忠指忠于国事，孝指在家里孝敬父母。但忠孝之间，往往有冲突，在家孝敬父母，就难以出来为国纾难；若是出来做官为国谋事，又不能时时在父母跟前侍奉，因此，古人常说“忠孝难两全”。此诗中的这个男子正是陷入了这种两难的困境。

69.A Lonely Callery Pear Tree

I climb the northern hill to pick wolfberries. I have to perform the never-ending military service for the sovereign, but I'm anxious about my parents at home. The chariot made of sandal wood is broken and the war horses are exhausted. I guess I will be allowed to go home in the near future.

From the 3rd Stanza of *Callery Pear Trees,*
Lesser Court Hymns, Classic of Poetry

【Commentary】

The poem is about the soldier on an expedition who misses his wife. It has four stanzas. The quoted stanza is about the soldier on an expedition who feels distressed at not being able to look after his parents. Ancient Chinese people attached great importance to loyalty to their sovereign and filial piety to their parents. However, it's hard for one to be both loyal and filial. If one wants to fulfill his filial duty, he can hardly leave his home and alleviate difficulties of his country for his sovereign. If one works as an official for the ruler, he can hardly stay at home and take care of his parents. The man in the poem is caught in the dilemma.

詩經選譯

鸿雁
Wild Geese

70．鸿雁

【原文】

鸿雁于飞，哀鸣嗷嗷。维此哲人，谓我劬劳。维彼愚人，谓我宣骄。

《诗经·小雅·鸿雁》三章

【释文】

大雁展翅高飞，它的哀鸣凄凉惨恻。只有明白事理的人，才能了解我的辛劳。而那些愚蠢的人，竟说我在炫耀排场。

【解析】

这是一首写周王派遣使臣救济难民的诗。诗共三章。诗歌以鸿雁飞于草野起兴，比喻使臣奔走四方。周宣王中兴，派遣使臣救济难民。但使臣的行为，却被人误解，因此心中郁闷。哀鸿一词，后来常常作为流民的代名词，就是从此诗引申出来的。

70.Wild Geese

Wild geese spread their wings to soar. They give mourning cries. Only sensible men can understand my hard work while those foolish people think I'm showing off.

From the 3rd Stanza of *Wild Geese,*
Lesser Court Hymns, Classic of Poetry

【Commentary】

The poem is about the king of Zhou who sent his emissaries to provide disaster relief to victims. It has three stanzas. The poet uses wild geese that spread wings to soar as affective images to refer to the emissaries who go hither and thither. The King Xuan of Zhou sent his emissaries to provide disaster relief to victims. Unfortunately, what they did was misconceived, so they felt depressed. "Wild geese that give mourning cries" have often been used as a byword for displaced people since then.

71. 鹤鸣

【原文】

鹤鸣于九皋，声闻于天。鱼在于渚，或潜在渊。乐彼之园，爰有树檀，其下维榖。它山之石，可以攻玉。

《诗经·小雅·鹤鸣》二章

【释文】

白鹤在曲折的沼泽中鸣叫，它的叫声响亮得传到天上。鱼在沙洲边自由遨游，有时又潜入深渊中。那个美丽快乐的花园里，种植了高大的檀树，也有矮小的楮树。别的山上的石头，可以用来琢磨玉器。

【解析】

这是一首抒发招纳人才为国所用的诗。诗共两章。诗以鹤鸣九皋、鱼潜深渊起兴，比喻人才有显隐之别，但都可以取为国用，不必拘限于本国。先秦时期，各诸侯国都有一些君王如魏文侯等，能够励精图治，向天下招揽人才。而当时人才流通也相对自由，因此有识之士往往能够吸纳他国人才为本国所用。

71.White Cranes Cry

White cranes cry in the swamp. Their cries are so loud that they pierce the sky. Fish swim freely along the shoal. Sometimes they dive into the abyss. In the beautiful garden that is filled with laughter, there are tall and big sandal trees as well as short and small paper mulberries. Stones from other mountains can be used to make jade ware.

From the 2nd Stanza of *White Cranes Cry,*
Lesser Court Hymns, Classic of Poetry

【Commentary】

The poem is about recruiting talents for the country. It has two stanzas. The poem uses white cranes that cry in the swamp and fish that dive into the abyss as affective images to show that some talents are conspicuous while others are hidden, but they can both be used for the sake of the country and not only local talents but also those who are from other countries can be used for the benefits of the country. In the pre-Qin period, rulers of vassal states like Marquess Wen of Wei exerted themselves to make their states prosperous. To achieve their ambition, they attracted talents from all around the world. As the flow of talents was free at that time, men of insight from other countries could be used.

詩經選譯

白驹

A White Pony

72. 白驹

【原文】

皎皎白驹，在彼空谷。生刍一束，其人如玉。毋金玉尔音，而有遐心。

《诗经·小雅·白驹》四章

【释文】

洁白的小马，在山谷里自由地奔跑。以一捆娇嫩的青草作礼物，期盼如玉一样高洁的朋友的到来。请不要吝惜你的音信，使我们彼此有疏远之心。

【解析】

这是一首别友思贤的诗。诗共四章。诗歌以白马来亲近主人起兴，反衬友人离别之后，音讯全无。“生刍一束”，指新割的青草，代指送给朋友的礼物；“其人如玉”，指朋友之德美如玉。两句诗说的是礼物虽轻，但待友之情却深厚之意。

72.A White Pony

A white pony is trotting freely in the valley. I give it a bundle of freshly cut grass as a gift with the hope that my friends who are as noble and unsullied as jade will come. Please do not grudge letting me know your news and do not estrange yourself from me.

From the 4th Stanza of *A White Pony,*
Lesser Court Hymns, Classic of Poetry

【Commentary】

The poem is about bidding farewell to one's good friends. It has four stanzas. The poem uses the white pony that is close to its master as an affective image to contrast with his friend who has not contacted him after parting. The "freshly cut grass" refers to gifts sent to one's friend and "as noble and unsullied as jade" refers to the virtue of one's friend. The two lines imply that although gifts are not expensive, one has a deep affection for his friend.

73. 斯干

【原文】

乃生男子，载寝之床，载衣之裳，载弄之璋。其泣喤喤，朱芾斯皇，室家君王。

《诗经·小雅·斯干》八章

【释文】

如果生了男孩，就给他睡大床，给他穿衣裳，给他玩玉璋。孩子的哭声洪亮，红色的礼服鲜艳华丽，将来不是做国君就是王。

【解析】

这是一首歌颂周王宫室建成的诗。诗共九章。诗歌写周王生儿子则给孩子穿衣玩玉，这与本诗第九章形成鲜明对比。第九章写生女儿则只用布被包裹，玩弄纺线用的陶制纺锤。后世以弄璋来代指生儿子，弄瓦代指生女儿，就源于此诗。古代中国人有强烈的宗族观念，往往认为儿子众多可以强大家族，提高家族的社会地位，因此比较宠爱儿子，这种男尊女卑观念反映在文学作品中，就以此诗为最早。

73.A Creek

If the forthcoming baby is a boy, please have him sleep on a big bed and dress him and give him jade tablets as toys. The boy is with loud howls and on gorgeous red gown. He will be an emperor or king after growing up.

From the 8th Stanza of *A Creek,*
Lesser Court Hymns, Classic of Poetry

【Commentary】

The poem eulogizes the newly built palace of Zhou. It has nine stanzas. The poem is about baby boys of the king who are dressed and given jade as toys. It is in stark contrast to the ninth stanza of the poem, which is about baby girls of the king who are wrapped by cloth and have nothing to play with but ceramic spindles. The later generations use "playing with jade tablets" to refer to boys while "playing with ceramic spindles" to mean girls. Ancient China was a patriarchal society, so sons were favored over daughters. It was believed that the more sons a family had, the more powerful it was and the more elevated social position it had. Such an idea was originated from a long time ago and the poem is the first literary work reflecting the idea.

詩經選譯

十月之交

Early the Tenth Lunar Month

74. 十月之交

【原文】

烨烨震电，不宁不令。百川沸腾，山冢崒崩。高岸为谷，深谷为陵。哀今之人，胡憯莫惩！

《诗经·小雅·十月之交》三章

【释文】

天上雷声轰鸣闪电不息，国家政治黑暗使百姓不得安宁。江海河川的水流奔腾不止，山崩地裂乱石纷飞。高山下降变成深谷，深谷上升变为丘陵。可悲的是现在的当权者，却不能引以为戒啊！

【解析】

这是一首讽刺周幽王无道致使人民受难的诗。诗共八章。诗歌开头写到“日有食之”，这是中国最早记载日食、月食的诗歌。全诗描写自然灾难，以喻社会的动荡变幻，把日食、月食、强烈的地震同朝廷用人不善联系起来，在中国文化史上，逐渐形成所谓的“天人感应”思想，即认为自然灾难和自然异象的出现与统治者的失德有关。“高岸为谷，深谷为陵”，这两句诗常常被后人用来比喻人世间的剧烈变化。

74.Early the Tenth Lunar Month

Thunders roar while lightning flashes. Common people find no peace against the backdrop of political darkness. Seas, rivers and lakes surge while rocks randomly fall after landslides. High mountains fall and become deep valleys while deep valleys rise and become hills. How pathetic the current rulers are! They cannot take all the phenomena as warnings.

From the 3rd Stanza of *Early the Tenth Lunar Month, Lesser Court Hymns, Classic of Poetry*

【Commentary】

The poem satirizes the fatuous King You of Zhou who caused his people to suffer. It has eight stanzas. The poem is the earliest of its kind to describe the eclipses of the sun and the moon. The natural disasters mentioned by the poem are metaphor of social unrest. The poet links eclipses of the sun and the moon and severe earthquakes with appointment of unqualified officials by the ruler. The idea that the nature interacts with human beings has been developed in the cultural history of China afterwards and the emergence of natural disasters and anomalies of the nature were believed to be linked with misconduct of rulers. The lines "high mountains fall and become deep valleys while deep valleys rise and become hills" are often used by later generations to refer to drastic social changes.

75. 小旻

【原文】

不敢暴虎，不敢冯河。人知其一，莫知其他。战战兢兢，如临深渊，如履薄冰。

《诗经·小雅·小旻》六章

【释文】

不敢徒手与老虎搏斗，不敢徒步涉过长河。人人都明白这个道理，却不懂其他危险。做任何事都要小心谨慎，就好像在深渊边上行走，像在薄冰上踩过一样。

【解析】

这是一首讽刺周幽王任用小人以致朝政昏乱的诗。诗共六章。中国人处事，讲究谋定而后动、三思而后行，诗歌以暴虎、冯河起兴，比喻莽撞行事之不可取。诗末三句尤其提醒人们，做任何事都要认真谨慎，才能防患于未然。

75.Despotic Heaven

People dare not fight tigers with their bare hands, nor cross rivers with their bare feet. People all know that they should avoid such dangers, but they do not know that there're other dangers. Do everything cautiously as if you were walking on the edge of an abyss or on thin ice.

From the 6th Stanza of *Despotic Heaven,*
Lesser Court Hymns, Classic of Poetry

【Commentary】

The poem satirizes King You of Zhou who appointed men of vile character to high positions, leading to administrative chaos. It has six stanzas. Chinese people like to think before acting, so the poem uses fighting tigers with their bare hands, or crossing rivers with their bare feet as affective images to show that it is inadvisable to act recklessly. The last three lines of the poem warn people to do everything cautiously in order to keep them from hidden dangers.

詩經選譯

小弁
Weighed down with Worry

76. 小弁

【原文】

维桑与梓，必恭敬止。靡瞻匪父，靡依匪母。不属于毛，不离于里。天之生我，我辰安在？

《诗经·小雅·小弁》三章

【释文】

对父母种植的桑梓树，我们也必须怀有恭敬心。没有人不恭敬父亲，没有人不依靠母亲。我的皮毛生于父亲，我的血肉连着母亲。上天既然生育了我，却为何让我命运不佳而遭父母放逐？

【解析】

这是一首抒发被父亲放逐、心中哀怨的诗。诗共八章。从诗本身所表述的内容来看，当是诗人的父亲听信了谗言，把他放逐，致使他幽怨哀伤、零泪悲怀。中国人重视孝道，父母虽有过错，作儿女的也不能因此而怨恨父母。此诗所写的情况，就反映了中国传统孝道的文化特质。而诗中桑梓是父母种于门前的树木，后来就成了故乡的代称。

76.Weighed down with Worry

We should treat mulberry trees grown by our parents with respect. All the human beings respect their fathers and count on their mothers. My skin and hair come from my father while my flesh and blood are connected with my mother. Oh, Heaven, since I have been born, why am I unluckily banished by my parents?

From the 3rd Stanza of *Weighed down with Worry, Lesser Court Hymns, Classic of Poetry*

【Commentary】

The poet expresses grief after being banished by his father. It has eight stanzas. Judging from the poem, the poet is banished by his father who has believed slanderous words, so he is so grieved that he breaks into tears. Ancient Chinese took filial duty seriously. Children could not bear grudge against their parents even if it were their parents who should be blamed. The poem reflects the traditional filial piety. "Mulberry trees grown by one's parents" have become a byword for one's hometown.

詩經選譯

巧言

Deceiving Words

77. 巧言

【原文】

奕奕寝庙，君子作之。秩秩大猷，圣人莫之。他人有心，予忖度之。跃跃毚兔，遇犬获之。

《诗经·小雅·巧言》四章

【释文】

高大雄伟的宫殿宗庙，是先王下令建成的。完善的典章制度，是圣人制订保留下来的。有人存心要破坏它，我能揣度猜测得到。狡猾的兔子跑得再快，碰到猎狗也会遭殃。

【解析】

这是一首讽刺统治者听信谗言而祸国殃民的诗。诗共六章。诗歌以先王所建宫殿、典章起兴，比喻优良的传统应当坚持，不应听信谗言而改弦更张。此章后两句用比喻的手法指出，诗人能够预先判断出谗言的危害，希望君王能善用贤臣，以消除谗言的破坏。

77.Deceiving Words

The tall and magnificent palaces and temples were built by orders of the former king. The sound institutions have been made and kept by sages. If someone attempts to destroy them, I can speculate. Though a sly hare can run very quickly, it will be doomed to die when encountering a hunting dog.

From the 4th Stanza of *Deceiving Words,*
Lesser Court Hymns, Classic of Poetry

【Commentary】

The poem satirizes rulers who believe deceiving words, wreaking havoc on the country and its people. It has six stanzas. The poem uses the palaces and institutions made by the former king as affective images to indicate that the sovereign should maintain fine traditions rather than believe deceiving words to cut loose from the past and make a new start. By using metaphors in the last two lines in the stanza, the poet states that he can speculate on the harm of deceiving words and expresses his hope that the sovereign can use virtuous men to repair damage by deceiving words.

78．巷伯

【原文】

彼谮人者，谁适与谋？取彼谮人，投畀豺虎。豺虎不食，投畀有北。有北不受，投畀有昊。

《诗经·小雅·巷伯》六章

【释文】

那个爱造谣的人，谁愿和他多说话？抓住那个造谣人，拿去喂豺狼和老虎。虎狼都不愿吃他，再丢到寒冷的北方。如果北方不愿接受他，就交给上天治他的罪。

【解析】

这是寺人孟子因遭受谗言受害而作的怨诗。诗共七章。这里用顶真排比的手法来加强对谗言者的愤怒。寺人是中国古代遭受过宫刑的宦官。

78.Xiangbo

Who is willing to talk with the rumor monger? Seize the rumor monger and feed him to wolves and tigers. Even wolves and tigers are unwilling to eat him, so throw him to the icy northern area. If the northern area is unwilling to have him, let him be punished by Heaven.

From the 6th Stanza of *Xiangbo,*

Lesser Court Hymns, Classic of Poetry

【Commentary】

The poem is written by Mengzi, a castrated official who expresses his deep resentment after being framed by rumor mongers. It has seven stanzas. The poet employs anadiplosis and parallelism to express his deep resentment against the rumor mongers.

79. 谷风

【原文】

习习谷风，维风及雨。将恐将惧，维予与女。将安将乐，女转弃予。

《诗经·小雅·谷风》首章

【释文】

山谷里的大风不停地吹，狂风暴雨漫天下。当初担惊受怕的日子，只有我为你分担忧愁。如今过上了安乐的日子，你竟狠心地抛弃我。

【解析】

这是一首弃妇诗。诗共三章。中国古代婚姻制度，使女子常常处于婚姻的不利困境中，甚至被抛弃。而妇女社会地位低下的现实，又使她们在面对遗弃时，大多没有更好的应对举措，只能在忧怨、悲愤中结束人生。

79.Gales from the Mountain Valley

Gales from the mountain valley are blowing with no end while heavy rain is pouring down. When you suffered great anxiety, it was only I who stayed by your side and shared your woes. How dare you abandon me after living a happy and prosperous life?

From the 1st Stanza of *Gales from the Mountain Valley,*
Lesser Court Hymns, Classic of Poetry

【Commentary】

The poem is about an abandoned wife. It has three stanzas. Women were under unfavorable situation and even were abandoned according to the ancient Chinese marriage institution. Due to their low social position, they could not have effective countermeasures and had to end their lives with resentment after being abandoned.

蓼莪

Tall Incarvillea Sinensis Lamarck

80. 蓼莪

【原文】

父兮生我，母兮鞠我。拊我畜我，长我育我，顾我复我，出入腹我。欲报之德，昊天罔极！

《诗经·小雅·蓼莪》四章

【释文】

父亲生养我，母亲哺育我。他们抚摸爱护我，养育教导我，照顾挂念我，进出都抱着我。如今我想报答父母的恩情，不料父母已双亡！

【解析】

这是一首苦于服役、悼念父母的诗。诗共六章。诗人因为长久在外服役，不能回来侍奉父母，等他回来时，父母已过世。诗歌不仅表达了对父母生养艰辛的感慨，更多的是悔恨内疚，这种情形就是中国俗语常说的“子欲养而亲不待”。

80. Tall Incarvillea Sinensis Lamarck

My father gave me life while my mother raised me. They loved me, taught me and took good care of me. They held me in their arms no matter we were at home or out. I want to repay my parents for their kindness, but they've already passed away.

From the 4th Stanza of *Tall Incarvillea Sinensis Lamarck, Lesser Court Hymns, Classic of Poetry*

【Commentary】

The poem is about the man who is fulfilling his corvee duty and missing his deceased parents. It has six stanzas. The poet could not look after his parents because he had to fulfill his corvee duty for a long time and when he came back home, he found that his parents had already passed away. The poet described the hardships suffered by his parents of raising him and expressed deep regret for unable to look after them. A Chinese saying goes that children want to take care of their parents, but they have died.

81. 大东

【原文】

维南有箕，不可以簸扬。维北有斗，不可以挹酒浆。维南有箕，载翕其舌。维北有斗，西柄之揭。

《诗经·小雅·大东》七章

【释文】

南方有箕星，却不能簸扬米糠。北边有北斗星，也不能舀酒浆。南方有箕星，却缩着大舌头。北边有北斗星，但它的柄却指向西方。

【解析】

这是一首东方诸侯国的臣民讽刺周王残暴不恤百姓的诗。诗共七章。诗以天上的北斗和南箕设喻，这些东西可看不能用，无法解决臣民的温饱。这反映了臣民对现实的不满。

81.Vassal States far from the Capital

There is Willowing Basket in the south, but it cannot winnow rice bran. There is Big Dipper in the north, but it cannot dip rice wine. There is Willowing Basket in the south, but it rolls its big tongue. There is Big Dipper in the north, but its handle points to the west.

From the 7th Stanza of *Vassal States far from the Capital,*
Lesser Court Hymns, Classic of Poetry

【Commentary】

The poem is about people of the eastern vassal states who satirized the ruthless king of Zhou. It has seven stanzas. The poem uses Big Dipper in the north and Willowing Basket in the south as metaphors to show that what can be seen but cannot be used cannot feed people. It reflects the discontent among people about the reality.

詩經選譯

北山

Northern Mountain

82. 北山

【原文】

溥天之下，莫非王土。率土之滨，莫非王臣。大夫不均，我从事独贤。

《诗经·小雅·北山》二章

【释文】

普天之下的土地，没有不是君王的领土。四海之内的人民，没有不是君王的臣民。大夫安排工作很不公平，给我的差事最艰苦。

【解析】

这是一首抱怨徭役不均的诗。诗共六章。诗歌谴责统治者的徭役繁重和不均，诗歌开头的四句，对中国人的思想影响尤大。中国古代人认为，天子代表国家，富有天下、臣民、土地，一切都属于天子。此诗强调周天子至高无上的地位，客观上也促成了中国古代多民族融合和大一统观念的形成。

82.Northern Mountain

All the territory under the heavens belongs to the sovereign. All the people within the four seas are his subjects. The high-ranking official is unfair when assigning jobs for he has given me the toughest one.

From the 2nd Stanza of *Northern Mountain,*
Lesser Court Hymns, Classic of Poetry

【Commentary】

The poem is about complaints about unequal assignment of corvee duties. It has six stanzas. The poem denounces the heavy and unequally assigned corvee duties imposed by rulers. The first four lines of the poem have profound influence on the thoughts of Chinese. Ancient Chinese held the belief that the sovereign represented the country and Heaven; people and land all belonged to the sovereign. The poem emphasizes the supreme position of the king of Zhou and it has facilitated the multi-ethnic integration and development of the idea about great unity.

83. 小明

【原文】

嗟尔君子！无恒安处。靖共尔位，正直是与。神之听之，式穀以女。

《诗经·小雅·小明》四章

【释文】

我的老朋友啊！请不要安于现状。做好你的本职工作，亲近正直贤良的人。神明看到你的努力，必定会赐予你福禄。

【解析】

这是一首官吏自述久役思归和念友的诗。诗共五章。此章是告诫老朋友要忠于本职工作，更要选贤授能，这样才能得到神明的保佑护持。中国人主张忠于其事，为人谋事而尽心尽力，做到无愧于天地良心。诗中“无恒安处”更有启示的意义，告诫人们不要安于现状，而要兢兢惕惕，居安思危。

83.A Dark Country

My old friend, do not be content with things as they are. Do your duty well and approach upright and virtuous men. Heaven will give you blessings after seeing your strenuous efforts.

From the 4th Stanza of *A Dark Country,*
Lesser Court Hymns, Classic of Poetry

【Commentary】

The poem is about the official who misses his home and his old friends after working far away from home for a long time. It has five stanzas. In the quoted stanza, the poet advises his old friend to do his duty well and use virtuous men so that he can be blessed by Heaven. Chinese hold the belief that one should conscientiously work for others. The line "do not be content with things as they are" is inspiring and it warns people against being content with the current situation and asks them to take precautions beforehand.

詩經選譯

车舝

Axle End Components

84. 车舝

【原文】

高山仰止，景行行止。四牡骓骓，六辔如琴。觏尔新昏，以慰我心。

《诗经·小雅·车舝》五章

【释文】

高山需要仰望才能看见山顶，平坦的大路则任人驰骋。驾着四匹马儿欢快地跑，抓着六根缰绳如调琴弦。我看见车上的新婚青年，心里也感觉欢喜和宽慰。

【解析】

这是一首诗人在迎娶途中所赋的诗。诗共五章。诗以高山大路起兴，比喻诗人见到这对新人的车马，内心为新人的幸福而欢欣鼓舞。“高山仰止，景行行止”这两句诗后来浓缩为成语“高山景行”，比喻人的崇高的品德。

84.Axle End Components

The top of the high mountain cannot be seen unless you lift your head while a level wide road allows all the people to use. I drive my carriage and the four horses trot briskly. I pull on the six reins, like tuning the strings. I feel happy and relieved seeing the newly married young couple in the carriage.

From the 5th Stanza of *Axle End Components,*
Lesser Court Hymns, Classic of Poetry

【Commentary】

The poet writes it on his way to marry his wife. It has five stanzas. The poet uses high mountains and broad roads as affective images to show that he is happy for the newly married young couple after seeing them in a carriage. The two lines "the top of the high mountain cannot be seen unless you lift your head while a level wide road allows all the people to use" have been shortened into an idiom "high mountains and wide roads", a metaphor for men of lofty moral character.

85. 青蝇

【原文】

营营青蝇，止于樊。岂弟君子，无信谗言。

《诗经·小雅·青蝇》首章

【释文】

嗡嗡叫的苍蝇到处飞舞，飞到篱笆才停下来。平易近人的君子，不要相信谗言。

【解析】

这是一首斥责谗人害人祸国的诗。诗共三章。诗歌以青蝇止于篱笆起兴，比喻谗言满天，希望君子不要听信谗言。“岂弟”就是“恺悌”，意思是和乐平易，泛指品德优良、平易近人的人。而诗中“青蝇”就成了谗言或进谗佞人的代称。

85.Flies

Flies buzz around before stopping on the fences. An affable man of noble character will not believe slanderous words.

From the 1st Stanza of *Flies,*
Lesser Court Hymns, Classic of Poetry

【Commentary】

The poem reprimands backbiters for inflicting harm on others and their country. It has three stanzas. The poem uses flies that stop on the fences as affective images in the beginning to refer to widespread slanderous words and expresses the hope that men of noble character will not believe them. “Flies” in the poem have become a byword for slanderous words or backbiters.

86. 角弓

【原文】

尔之远矣，民胥然矣。尔之教矣，民胥效矣。

《诗经·小雅·角弓》二章

【释文】

你如果疏远了亲属，人民也会跟着你变坏。你假如教导他们向善，人民也会效仿你变好。

【解析】

这是一首劝告王公贵族不要疏远兄弟亲戚而亲近小人的诗。诗共八章。这一章写王公贵族的言行举止对百姓的影响。中国古代虽有司徒之官以掌教化，引导百姓行善明礼，但总体而言，普通百姓没有什么知识文化，他们往往会以王公贵族和官员的话语行为作榜样而亦步亦趋，所以诗人对此多有警示，希望统治者能积德导善，以作榜样。

86.Bows Made of Ox Horns

If you estrange yourself from your relatives, your people will follow suit and become evil. If you direct them to be good, they will emulate you and become good.

From the 2nd Stanza of *Bows Made of Ox Horns,*
Lesser Court Hymns, Classic of Poetry

【Commentary】

The poem advises aristocrats against estranging them from their siblings and relatives to approach the mean men. It has eight stanzas. The quoted stanza is about the influence of what aristocrats do on the common people. Although there were officials who were in charge of guiding the common people to behave in accordance with rites, the poorly educated common people liked to follow the example of aristocrats and officials. So the poet advised the ruling class to be virtuous and become role models for common people.

詩經選譯

采绿

Pick Herbs of Hispid Arthraxon

87. 采绿

【原文】

终朝采绿，不盈一匊。予发曲局，薄言归沐。

《诗经·小雅·采绿》首章

【释文】

整个早晨都在采荩草，却采不满一捧草。我的头发又卷又曲，我还是赶紧回家洗头去。

【解析】

这是一首妇女思念外出的丈夫的诗。诗共四章。丈夫逾期不归，她无心采荩，也无心打扮。诗歌以两个细节写出这位妇女内心的不平静：整整一个早上的时间，却采不满一捧的草，那是因为思念着丈夫，无心采摘；头发散乱没有洗梳，也同样是因为思念而无心修饰。

87.Pick Herbs of Hispid Arthraxon

I spent the whole morning picking herbs of hispid arthraxon, but all I had was only a handful of them. My hair is disheveled, so I'd better rush home and wash my hair.

From the 1st Stanza of *Pick Herbs of Hispid Arthraxon, Lesser Court Hymns, Classic of Poetry*

【Commentary】

The poem is about the wife who misses her husband. It has four stanzas. She is in no mood to pick herbs of hispid arthraxon or dress up. The poem describes the restlessness of the lady with two details: she spent the whole morning picking herbs of hispid arthraxon, but all she had was only a handful of them because she misses her husband so desperately that she is in no mood to pick herbs. Her hair is disheveled because she misses her husband so dreadfully that she is in no mood to dress her hair.

88. 隰桑

【原文】

心乎爱矣，遐不谓矣？中心藏之，何日忘之？

《诗经·小雅·隰桑》四章

【释文】

我的心里深爱着你，为什么总是不告诉你呢？我心中深藏着对你的思念之情，哪一天能忘得了？

【解析】

这是一首妇女思念丈夫的诗。诗共四章。诗中女子面对丈夫时，不能直白地表露对丈夫的爱，只能藏于心底，但却不会忘记，情感表达虽含蓄却真挚深沉。

88.Mulberry Trees in the Low-lying Wetland

I am crazy about you, but why haven't I expressed my love for you? I miss you terribly. How can I forget you for even one day?

From the 4th Stanza of *Mulberry Trees in the Low-lying Wetland, Lesser Court Hymns, Classic of Poetry*

【Commentary】

The poem is about the wife who misses her husband. It has four stanzas. When facing her husband, the wife is too shy to express her love for him. She has to bury her love deeply in her heart. Her feelings are implicit but genuine and deep.

詩經選譯

何草不黄

What Type of Grass Does Not Wither and Turn Yellow

89. 何草不黄

【原文】

何草不黄？何日不行？何人不将？经营四方。

《诗经·小雅·何草不黄》首章

【释文】

哪一种草不枯黄？哪一天不忙活？哪一个人不出征？我们总是不停地在四方奔走。

【解析】

这是一首征夫哀叹行役的诗。诗共四章。周代徭役繁杂沉重，种类繁多，但大致可以归纳成力役和兵役两种。统治者频繁征调民力，使平民苦不堪言，因而怨声载道。

89.What Type of Grass Does Not Wither and Turn Yellow

What type of grass does not wither and turn yellow? On which day can we be idle? Who can be free from military expeditions? We have to work hard all day.

From the 1st Stanza of *What Type of Grass Does Not Wither and Turn Yellow, Lesser Court Hymns, Classic of Poetry*

【Commentary】

The poem is the lament of people who do corvee duties. It has four stanzas. In Zhou Dynasty, there were numerous types of heavy corvee duties, which could be classified into two types: labor and military duties. The ruling class frequently mobilized common people to do corvee duties, making them suffer a lot and complain bitterly.

90. 文王

【原文】

文王在上，於昭于天。周虽旧邦，其命维新。有周不显，帝命不时。文王陟降，在帝左右。

《诗经·大雅·文王》首章

【释文】

文王的神明高高在上，在天上大放光明。岐周虽然是古老的邦国，但接受天命建立新王朝。周朝的前途无限，遵照上天赋予的使命。文王的神明升到了天上，就在上帝的左右旁。

【解析】

这是一首诗人追述文王事迹以告诫成王的诗。诗共七章。诗中写周民族虽是一个古老的民族，有悠久的历史，但它能创新，因此具有顽强的生命力。西周民族起源于中国西北，其始祖后稷在尧时被任命为管理农业的官员，其后经过几百年繁衍，至文王姬昌时，逐渐发展成为与殷商王朝抗衡的新兴强国。此后武王继承文王的事业，一举剿灭残暴无道的殷商王朝，建立了相对开明的西周政权。西周制订的一系列典章文化制度，一直影响到中国人今天生活的方方面面。

90.King Wen of Zhou

The spirit of King Wen is in Heaven and shines brightly. Though with a long history, Zhou people followed the mandate of Heaven to establish a new dynasty. By following the mandate of Heaven, the Zhou Dynasty has a bright future. The spirit of King Wen has ascended to Heaven and stood beside Heavenly Deity.

From the 1st Stanza of *King Wen of Zhou,*
Major Court Hymns, Classic of Poetry

【Commentary】

The poet cautioned King Cheng by recounting exploits of King Wen. It has seven stanzas. Although the Zhou race has a long history, it is of tremendous vitality due to innovation. The Western Zhou race originated from northwestern China, and its ancestor Houji was appointed the official in charge of farming during the reign of Yao. Since then, after several hundred years' development, it became a powerful state to confront the Shang Dynasty during the reign of King Wen. King Wu succeeded King Wen to the throne. He overthrew the Shang Dynasty and put an end to the despotic ruling and established the enlightened Western Zhou Dynasty. Institutions made in the Western Zhou Dynasty still affect Chinese people today.

詩經選譯

旱麓
The Foot of Han Mountain

91. 旱麓

【原文】

鸢飞戾天，鱼跃于渊。岂弟君子，遐不作人？

《诗经·大雅·旱麓》三章

【释文】

老鹰飞到天上去，鱼儿跳跃到深潭里。平易近人的君子，为什么不培养人才呢？

【解析】

这是一首歌颂周文王祭祖得福、培养人才的诗。诗共六章。诗以鹞鹰展翅、鱼儿跃渊起兴，比喻恺悌之士能够培养青年、提携后学。周王朝的兴盛，就得益于人才的重用和培养，周文王、周武王重用姜太公，印证了此诗所叙写的用贤育才事实。

91.The Foot of Han Mountain

Eagles fly to the sky while fish dive into deep pools. Oh, affable men of noble character, why don't you cultivate talents?

From the 3rd Stanza of *The Foot of Han Mountain,*

Major Court Hymns, Classic of Poetry

【Commentary】

The poem eulogizes King Wen of Zhou who was blessed by making sacrifices to his ancestors and devoted his attention to cultivating talents. It has six stanzas. The poem uses eagles that fly to the sky and fish that dive into deep pools as affective images to show that affable men of noble character cultivate young people. The rise of the Zhou Dynasty benefited from cultivation and use of talents. Kings Wen and Wu put Jiang Ziya in an important position, which is a good example of using virtuous men mentioned by the poem.

92. 思齐

【原文】

惠于宗公，神罔时怨，神罔时恫。刑于寡妻，至于兄弟，以御于家邦。

《诗经·大雅·思齐》二章

【释文】

文王能够敬顺祖宗，祖宗没有埋怨，祖宗也没有伤心过。文王以礼仪贤德成为妻子的榜样，也是兄弟的模范，进而以此治理国家。

【解析】

这是一首歌颂文王善于修身、齐家、治国的诗。诗共五章。诗歌写文王以礼待妻、兄弟，并以此治国而国事亨通。国家并称，大则为国，小则治家，古人相信，治理家国的道理都是相通的，所以后人说“求忠臣必于孝子之门”，正与此诗异曲同工。

92.The Dignified Mother

King Wen showed filial obedience to his older generation, so they never complained or felt distressed. King Wen set an example for his wife and his siblings by observing rites and showing virtue. Thanks to such qualities, he was able to rule his country well.

From the 2nd Stanza of *The Dignified Mother,*
Major Court Hymns, Classic of Poetry

【Commentary】

The poem eulogizes King Wen who was good at cultivating himself, managing his family and ruling his country. According to the poem, King Wen treated his wife and siblings and ruled his country in accordance with rites, so his country was in peace and prosperity. The ancients held the belief that ruling a country was like managing a family. Therefore, the later generations had such a saying: a loyal official must be a filial son, which coincided with the poem.

詩經選譯

生民

Birth of Houji

93. 生民

【原文】

厥初生民，时维姜嫄。生民如何？克禋克祀，以弗无子。履帝武敏歆，攸介攸止。载震载夙，载生载育，时维后稷。

《诗经·大雅·生民》首章

【释文】

当初周民族的祖先能出生，都是因为姜嫄淑德贤惠。她是怎么生下周民的始祖的呢？她虔诚地祷告神灵与上天，乞求怀孕生子。此后她就踩了天帝的拇趾印，得到神灵的保佑和恩赐。怀孕时精心呵护胎儿，勤劳养育新生儿，这个孩子就是周人的祖先后稷。

【解析】

这是一首叙写周民族始祖后稷神奇事迹的诗。诗共八章。周民族有久远的历史，经过十几代人的苦心经营，至周武王时灭商，建立周王朝。其后代子孙追述祖先创业的艰辛，旨在表彰祖宗的功业，也是期待得到祖宗的保佑、庇护与恩赐。

93.Birth of Houji

The ancestor of Zhou people could be born because Jiangyuan was virtuous. How did Jiangyuan give birth to the ancestor of Zhou? She prayed to Heaven for conceiving a son and treaded on the thumbprint of Heavenly Deity, so she was blessed by divinities. She took care of the fetus when pregnant and devoted her energy to parenting her new-born baby. The child was the ancestor of Zhou.

From the 1st Stanza of *Birth of Houji,*
Major Court Hymns, Classic of Poetry

【Commentary】

The poem is about the amazing story of Houji, the ancestor of Zhou. It has eight stanzas. Zhou people enjoyed a long history. After a dozen of generations' hard work, Zhou people overthrew Shang and established Zhou Dynasty under the leadership of King Wu. The offspring of Zhou recounted the hardships of pioneering work endured by their ancestors with the aim of honoring their exploits and getting their blessings.

詩經選譯

公刘

Gongliu

94．公刘

【原文】

笃公刘，匪居匪康。迺埸迺疆，迺积迺仓。迺裹糇粮，于橐于囊。思辑用光，弓矢斯张。干戈戚扬，爰方启行。

《诗经·大雅·公刘》首章

【释文】

笃实忠厚的公刘，不敢安居图享受。带领周人划分疆界耕种田地，收获粮食装入仓库。准备食物作为干粮，装入小袋和大囊。公刘带领大家团结一致争光荣，佩上弓箭武装起来。拿好盾戈斧钺，奋勇争先向前进。

【解析】

这是一首叙述周人祖先公刘带领周人由邰迁豳的诗。诗共六章。此篇与《大雅·生民》《大雅·绵》一起构成了周人史诗系列。公刘是后稷的曾孙，他带领流落于戎狄的部族迁居于豳地，从事农业生产、开拓疆土、厚积民德，使周民族初具邦国气象。

94.Gongliu

Honest and loyal Gongliu, he did not dare to indulge in pleasure. He led Zhou people to demarcate boundaries and till the land and harvest crops and store them in barns. He prepared solid food and put it in pockets and sacks. Gongliu united Zhou people to fight for glory. Armed with bows and arrows, shields, dagger-axes, axes and battle-axes, they courageously strived to be the first to confront their enemies.

From the 1st Stanza of *Gongliu,*
Major Court Hymns, Classic of Poetry

【Commentary】

The poem is about Gongliu, the ancestor of Zhou people who led his people to move their home from Tai to Bin. It has six stanzas. It is the epic series of Zhou people together with another two poems in the Major Court Hymns *Birth of Houji* and *Long Melon Vines*. Gongliu was the great-grandson of Houji. He led his people who were stranded in the land of western and northern nomads to Bin and engage in farming, expand their territory and build up virtue, laying a solid foundation for the Zhou descendants to establish their country.

95. 板

【原文】

上帝板板，下民卒瘅。出话不然，为犹不远。靡圣管管，不实于亶。犹之未远，是用大谏。

《诗经·大雅·板》首章

【释文】

国君昏乱乖戾反常，百姓因此辛劳疲病。说出的话都不合理，制定的政策没有远见。一意孤行不尊重贤人，言不由衷缺少诚信。你治理国家没有远见，因此我要劝谏你。

【解析】

这是一首劝告厉王施行仁政的诗。诗共八章。周人以举贤授能立国，周朝要想绵延传承下去，也需要贤能的辅佐。但西周末年，厉王抛弃祖宗规制，背离先人道德，倒行逆施，对敢言者采取监视和屠杀的严厉手段，最终导致国家的覆灭。

95.Surly and Perverse

The ruler is surly and perverse, so his people have suffered badly. What he says is unreasonable and policies he made are short-sighted. He acts in disregard of the virtuous men's opinions and he says one thing but means another. I admonish him for lacking foresight in ruling his country.

From the 1st Stanza of *Surly and Perverse,*
Major Court Hymns, Classic of Poetry

【Commentary】

The poem exhorts King Li to exercise benevolent governance. It has eight stanzas. Zhou people established their country with the support of virtuous and able men and virtuous officials were the necessity for sustaining the dynasty. Nevertheless, in the late Western Zhou Dynasty, King Li abandoned institutions and moral standards established by his ancestors. He had those who dared to criticize him monitored and killed. His perverse acts led to destruction of his country.

詩經選譯

蕩

Arrogant and Dissipated

96．荡

【原文】

文王曰咨，咨女殷商！人亦有言："颠沛之揭，枝叶未有害，本实先拨。"殷鉴不远，在夏后之世。

《诗经·大雅·荡》八章

【释文】

当年文王心中曾经有感慨，叹息殷商末代君王的昏乱！古人也曾这样说："树木拔倒露出了树根，枝叶虽然暂时没有受伤，但树根已经被破坏。"殷商覆灭的教训并不遥远，就在夏桀的时代。

【解析】

这是一首诗人哀伤厉王无道、周室将亡的诗。诗共八章。诗歌回忆文王曾经对殷商贵族的告诫之语，以此规劝周王。诗末"殷鉴不远，在夏后之世"两句，提醒周王要借鉴历史，从历史上的兴衰成败来检讨治国的策略，这形成中国源远流长的鉴古知今传统。

96.Arrogant and Dissipated

King Wen sighed at the thought of how tyrannical the last ruler of the Shang Dynasty was. The ancients said that stumps appeared after trees were felled. Although leaves were unscathed for a short while, stumps had already been damaged. The lessons of the destruction of Shang should not be forgotten in a not too long time. It happened not long after the collapse of Xia.

From the 8th Stanza of *Arrogant and Dissipated,*
Major Court Hymns, Classic of Poetry

【Commentary】

The poet was grieved to see that the Zhou Dynasty was on the verge of destruction due to tyrannical ruling by King Li. It has eight stanzas. The poet used words of caution by King Wen to aristocrats of Shang to exhort King Li. The lines "the lessons of the destruction of Shang should not be forgotten in a not too long time. It happened not long after the collapse of Xia" were used to remind King Li of drawing historical lessons and reviewing his ruling strategies from the perspective of historical successes and failures. It has created a precedent for Chinese people to learn from history.

97. 抑

【原文】

质尔人民，谨尔侯度，用戒不虞。慎尔出话，敬尔威仪，无不柔嘉。白圭之玷，尚可磨也。斯言之玷，不可为也！

《诗经·大雅·抑》五章

【释文】

安定你的人民，谨慎遵守法度，以防灾祸的突然发生。说话一定要谨慎，行为举止必须端正，为人和善友好。如果白玉上有斑点，还可以磨干净。要是开口不慎说错话，想要挽回就不可能了！

【解析】

这是一首周王朝老臣劝告、讽刺周王的诗。诗共十二章。诗以白玉有玷容易清除设喻，规劝周王要谨慎言行，因为君王的所作所为往往影响着国家的大政方针。中国人自古以来就有尊老敬贤的传统，认为这些宿老耆旧承载了古人累积的智慧与经验，大则可资治国，小则有益修身。他们对新人新事的指点、导向，往往有先见先觉的功效。

97.Cautious and Dignified

Make your people enjoy their life and cautiously observe institutions and prevent disasters from suddenly occurring. Be cautious with your words and behave well and treat others nicely. Spots on a piece of white jade can be erased. However, improper remarks that have been made cannot be taken back.

From the 5th Stanza of *Cautious and Dignified, Major Court Hymns, Classic of Poetry*

【Commentary】

The poem is about senior officials of Zhou who exhorted their king. It has twelve stanzas. The poet used spots on a piece of white jade that can be erased as a metaphor to exhort the king of Zhou to speak and act cautiously for what the sovereign said and did would influence the overall interest of the country. Chinese people have always followed the tradition of respecting the aged and the virtuous for their rich experience and profound wisdom. Their experience and wisdom are helpful in ruling a country and cultivating oneself. They have the foresight to provide guidance to newcomers and new things.

詩經選譯

桑柔

Young Mulberry Leaves

98. 桑柔

【原文】

国步蔑资，天不我将。靡所止疑，云徂何往？君子实维，秉心无竞。谁生厉阶？至今为梗。

《诗经·大雅·桑柔》三章

【释文】

国运艰难民生困苦，上天也不肯帮助我们。没有居住的地方，我们该往何处去？我们都在反思，我们没有争权夺利的想法。是谁制造这些祸端？至今还在为害人民。

【解析】

这是周厉王的大臣芮良夫讽刺厉王的诗。诗共十六章。西周末年，厉王无道，导致国危政乱，但诗人却明知故问，可知是痛恨太甚。而诗中“厉阶”一语也成为后来祸乱的代称。

98. Young Mulberry Leaves

Our country and we people are having hard times. Even Heaven is unwilling to help us. With no dwelling places, where should we go? We are reflecting and we have no intention of seizing power. Who has caused the catastrophes? We people have suffered a lot.

From the 3rd Stanza of *Young Mulberry Leaves,*
Major Court Hymns, Classic of Poetry

【Commentary】

The poem is about Rui Liangfu, the official of Zhou who satirized King Li. It has 16 stanzas. In the late Western Zhou Dynasty, the country was plunged into political chaos because of the tyrannical King Li, but the poet asked while knowing the answer, from which we can see that the poet loathed his king deeply.

99. 烝民

【原文】

天生烝民，有物有则。民之秉彝，好是懿德。天监有周，昭假于下。保兹天子，生仲山甫。

《诗经·大雅·烝民》首章

【释文】

上天养育了天下的人民，万事万物也都有法则。人们都有共同的禀赋，他们都喜欢美好的品德。上天观察周王朝，看到周王虔诚地祈祷。它保佑我大周天子，因此生下仲山甫来做辅佐的大臣。

【解析】

这是尹吉甫送别仲山甫的诗。诗共八章。宣王中兴，有贤臣辅佐，而仲山甫就是其中最出色的一位。他受宣王之命到齐地筑城，临别时又得好友尹吉甫作此诗赞美。这一章从万物都有法则说起，认为仲山甫是一位贤良之人，因此才能得到百姓的爱戴，帮助宣王中兴。诗中提到好善是人的本性，影响深远。

99.People under the Heavens

Heaven nurtures its people. The nature has its own law. Human beings share the same endowments and all value virtues. Heaven watches Zhou Dynasty and notices that its king has prayed earnestly. Zhong Shanfu was born as a blessing of Heaven for the king of Zhou.

From the 1st Stanza of *People under the Heavens, Major Court Hymns, Classic of Poetry*

【Commentary】

The poem is about Yin Jifu who saw off Zhong Shanfu. It has eight stanzas. King Xuan revived his country with the assistance of virtuous officials, among whom Zhong Shanfu was the most outstanding. Zhong Shanfu was ordered by the king to build a city in the Qi territory and he was praised by his good friend Yin Jifu before setting off. The quoted stanza of the poem starts from the nature that has its own law to show that Zhong Shanfu was a virtuous man, so he was loved by his people and committed himself to assisting King Xuan in reviving the country. The idea presented in the poem that "pursuit of goodness is man's nature" has profound influence.

詩經選譯

噫嘻

Pray to Heaven

100. 噫嘻

【原文】

噫嘻成王，既昭假尔。率时农夫，播厥百谷。骏发尔私，终三十里。亦服尔耕，十千维耦。

《诗经·周颂·噫嘻》首章

【释文】

成王轻声地祈祷，他向天神表达虔诚的敬意。他带领农夫一起到地里耕耘，安排农夫播种百谷。他要求百姓抓紧时间耕种官田和私田，这三十里的耕田要尽快完成。田官也要参与耕作，万民一起共同劳作。

【解析】

这是周成王春天祈谷的诗。诗共一章。周民族以农业立国，重视农业发展。作为国家最高统治者，天子必须在立春或立春后的吉日举行祭神祈谷之礼，然后带领官员象征性地到田里亲自耕作以劝勉百姓，宣告一年春耕的开始。农业生产，必得遵循春生、夏长、秋收、冬藏的自然规律，天子祈谷亲耕之举，是期待国泰民安，百姓在开春时辛勤劳作，才能春华秋实。周人文化影响中国后世极大，他们的这一文化传统也同样影响了中国后来的历代王朝。

100.Pray to Heaven

King Cheng prays quietly. He pays homage to Heavenly Deity. He leads peasants to till the land and directs them to grow crops. He asks his people to seize the time to cultivate both official land and private land. The 30-li long land should be ploughed as soon as possible. Land officials should join peasants in farming.

From the 1st Stanza of *Pray to Heaven, Sacrificial Odes of Zhou, Classic of Poetry*

【Commentary】

The poem is about King Cheng who prayed for spring plowing. It has one stanza. Agriculture was the foundation of the Zhou people, so they attached great importance to it. As the supreme ruler of the country, the king should perform the ceremony to offer sacrifices to Heaven and pray for spring plowing on the solar term "spring commences" or an auspicious day after it. After the ceremony, the king would lead his officials to symbolically till the land, a move to announce the beginning of spring plowing. Farming should follow such law: planting seeds in spring, growing in summer, harvesting in autumn and storing grain in winter. By personally praying for spring plowing, the king expected to see prosperity of the country and of its people. Hard work in spring would bring in bumper harvest in autumn. The culture of Zhou people has its profound influence upon the later generations and the following dynasties.